SLIGHTLY MORE GOOD THAN HARM

— · —

THE ETHAN CALDWELL STORIES

TREY NANTZ

CAROLOPOLIS
PRESS

CAROLOPOLIS PRESS

Contents

1

EPIGRAPH

"We do our jobs. We try to make good calls with bad information. And maybe, if we're lucky, we do slightly more good than harm."

2

— · —

PROLOGUE

E than Caldwell was twenty-five years old when he signed the contract with MVM, Inc.

The son of a State Department officer and a Savannah history teacher, he'd grown up between worlds—American suburbs and foreign postings, Southern values and global politics. At the College of Charleston, he'd studied international relations and caught the attention of Judge Alex Sterling, the former Chief Judge of the South Carolina Court of Appeals who'd returned to teaching after losing a Senate race.

Sterling had become his mentor. When Ethan finished law school at Charleston School of Law in May 2008, Sterling had made a call—to a contact from his time at Harvard's Kennedy School, to a contractor who needed smart analysts with legal training for operations in Iraq.

"Public service takes many forms," Sterling had told him. "Not all of them conventional."

Three months later, Ethan stepped off a C-130 into the furnace heat of Baqubah, Iraq. He carried an M4 rifle he barely knew how to use, wore body armor that felt like it weighed a thousand pounds, and had a job he didn't fully understand.

Intelligence analyst. Compliance observer. The guy who made sure operations followed the rules.

The team just called him "counselor."

He hadn't taken the bar exam yet. Wouldn't until February. But he had a law degree, a Harvard certificate, and enough understanding of the Geneva Conventions to keep operators out of congressional hearings.

That would have to be enough.

Six months. That was the contract. August 2008 to February 2009. Then he'd go home, take the bar, and start a normal legal career.

That was the plan.

He thought he'd signed up to keep others in line. He didn't realize the first person he'd lose control over was himself.

Iraq had other ideas.

3

FIRST DAY

The heat hit Ethan Caldwell like a physical assault the moment he stepped off the C-130. It wasn't just hot—that word was inadequate. It was 118 degrees of dry, relentless furnace heat that sucked the moisture from his lungs and made his eyes burn. Even at 0600, even with the sun barely up, Iraq felt like standing too close to an open oven.

"Keep moving! Off the bird!" A contractor in body armor and wraparound sunglasses was shouting, herding the new arrivals away from the aircraft. "Welcome to scenic Baqubah! Try not to die!"

Ethan shouldered his duffel—packed according to the list MVM had sent him: civilian clothes, toiletries, nothing that identified him as American—and followed the line of contractors and soldiers off the flight line. His polo shirt was already soaked through with sweat. His khakis stuck to his legs. The body armor they'd issued him at Ali Al Salem Air Base in Kuwait felt like it weighed a thousand pounds.

Twenty-five years old. Three months out of law school. Harvard Kennedy School certificate on his wall back in Charleston. And absolutely, completely, terrifyingly out of his depth.

"First time?" The guy next to him was maybe thirty, built like a fire hydrant, with the kind of tan that came from years in the sun, not a week at Myrtle Beach.

"That obvious?" Ethan managed.

"You're wearing khakis." The guy grinned. "Nobody wears khakis here unless they're brand new or desperately stupid. I'm Kozlowski. Team 3, but I'm with the task force element. You the new legal guy?"

"Ethan Caldwell. And yeah. Legal oversight."

"Oversight." Kozlowski laughed, not unkindly. "That's a nice way of saying 'make sure we don't violate the Geneva Conventions.' Don't worry, counselor. We mostly don't."

They were herded into a waiting area—a plywood structure with minimal air conditioning that nonetheless felt like paradise after the flight line. Ethan collapsed onto a bench and tried to process where he was.

Iraq. Actually Iraq. Not a training scenario. Not a case study from his Harvard program. The real thing.

The room smelled like sweat and gun oil and something else he couldn't identify—dust, maybe, or smoke, or the accumulated scent of thousands of men who'd passed through this same space on their way to war.

"Caldwell?" A staff sergeant with a clipboard appeared. "Ethan Caldwell?"

"Here."

"Come with me. We'll get you processed, issued your kit, and get you settled in your CHU."

"My what?"

"Containerized Housing Unit. Shipping container with AC and a bed. Home sweet home."

Ethan followed the sergeant through a maze of plywood buildings, concrete barriers, and sand-colored tents. The FOB was bigger than he'd expected—a small city, really, with designated areas marked by hand-painted signs: "TOC," "Chow Hall," "Latrines," "MWR." Soldiers and contractors moved with purpose, most in full kit despite the heat, rifles slung casually across their chests.

Everyone looked competent. Professional. Like they belonged here. Ethan felt like an imposter in khakis.

The issue point was controlled chaos. A bored-looking supply sergeant handed Ethan items from a list: rifle (M4 carbine with a serial number he was supposed to memorize), magazines (six of them, empty), ammunition (210 rounds of 5.56mm), and a bewildering array of other gear he didn't recognize.

"Sign here. Here. And here." The sergeant pushed forms across the counter. "Don't lose any of this shit. You break it, you bought it. Rifle stays with you at all times. At. All. Times. That clear?"

"Clear," Ethan said, looking at the M4 in his hands. He'd qualified with one during contractor training in Virginia—two weeks of basic weapons handling, first aid, and cultural awareness that now seemed laughably insufficient. But qualifying on a range in Virginia was different from carrying an actual weapon in an actual war zone.

"You know how to use that thing?" the sergeant asked, eyeing him skeptically.

"I qualified."

"That's not what I asked."

Ethan looked at the rifle. Safety selector switch. Magazine release. Charging handle. Bolt catch. He knew the parts. Knew the manual of arms. Could field strip and reassemble it in under two minutes.

But did he know how to *use* it? To actually point it at another human being and pull the trigger?

"I guess we'll find out," Ethan said.

The sergeant's expression softened slightly. "Stick close to your team. Do what they tell you. Most importantly, don't do anything stupid. Iraq's dangerous enough without adding stupid to the mix."

His CHU was a metal box in a long row of metal boxes, each one eight feet by twenty feet, each one containing a cot, a small desk, a mini-fridge, and a wall-mounted AC unit that wheezed heroically against the heat. The previous occupant had left a few items: a torn Tom Clancy novel, a pin-up calendar from 2007, and a hand-written note taped to the desk that said "Good luck, you'll need it."

Ethan dropped his duffel on the cot and sat down heavily. The AC was losing its battle with the Iraqi summer. Even inside, it had to be ninety degrees.

He looked at the rifle propped against the desk. His rifle now. The safety was on—he'd checked three times—but it still made him nervous just being in the same room with it.

His phone buzzed. No signal, but he had WiFi. An email from his mother: *Thinking of you. Be safe. Love you.*

He'd told his parents he was doing legal consulting work for an international development firm. Contract review, compliance monitoring, that sort of thing. They'd been proud but confused about why it required going to Iraq.

He hadn't mentioned the rifle. Or the body armor. Or the fact that he'd signed a contract acknowledging he might be injured or killed in the performance of his duties.

Another email, this one from Judge Sterling: *Ethan – Heard you made it safely. Remember what we discussed: public service takes many forms, not all of them conventional. Trust your judgment. Stay safe. – AS*

Ethan smiled despite everything. Their conversation in Charleston three months ago had been the thing that finally convinced him to take the MVM job. Sterling had talked about his own unconventional path—from lawyer to judge to politician to law school founder. About how the straight line wasn't always the right line.

"You're young," Sterling had said. "You've got time to do things the traditional way. But if you're going to do something different, do it now. While you still can. While you're still hungry enough to not care that it's uncomfortable."

Well, it was definitely uncomfortable.

A knock on his door. Ethan opened it to find Kozlowski and another man—late thirties, Hispanic, with the quiet confidence of someone who'd done this before.

"Caldwell? I'm Staff Sergeant Ramos. I run the team you're attached to. Kozlowski said you made it in okay."

"Yeah. Just getting settled."

Ramos looked past him at the unpacked duffel, the rifle that clearly hadn't been touched since it was issued. "You eaten?"

"Not since Kuwait."

"Chow hall's open. Come on, we'll get you fed and give you the brief on how things work around here."

Ethan grabbed his rifle—awkwardly, self-consciously—and followed them out into the Iraqi heat.

The chow hall was a large tent with industrial fans that did little except push hot air around. But the food was real—eggs, bacon, toast, coffee that was strong enough to stand a spoon in. Ethan loaded a tray and followed Ramos and Kozlowski to a table in the back.

"So," Ramos said, cutting into his eggs, "you're our new analyst guy. MVM sent your file. Says you went to Charleston Law, did some program at Harvard, taking the bar in February. That right?"

"That's right."

"And before that? Military experience? Law enforcement? Anything that prepares you for this?"

"No. Political science undergrad. Law school. That's it."

Ramos and Kozlowski exchanged a look.

"Okay," Ramos said. "So here's how this works. Our team does support for task force operations—raids, captures, intelligence gathering. Your job is to observe, document, and make sure we're following ROE and detainee handling protocols. You're not an operator. You're not expected to kick doors or clear rooms. But you need to be able to keep up, stay out of the way, and not get yourself or anyone else killed. That clear?"

"Clear."

"You'll carry that rifle everywhere. On base, off base, doesn't matter. It stays with you. You'll also carry your body armor, helmet, and basic load of ammunition. When we go outside the wire, you'll do exactly what I tell you, when I tell you. No questions, no hesitation. Lives depend on people doing what they're told when they're told. Understood?"

"Understood."

"Good." Ramos ate more eggs. "We've got a mission brief at 1400. Target package came in last night—suspected AQI safe house in sector. We'll hit it tonight around 0200. You'll come along, observe the detainee handling, make sure everything's documented properly. Consider it your welcome to Iraq."

Ethan's stomach dropped. Tonight. His first night. Less than twelve hours after arriving, he'd be going outside the wire on an actual operation.

"Any questions?" Ramos asked.

About a thousand. But Ethan just shook his head.

"He's got questions," Kozlowski said, grinning. "He's just too scared to ask them."

"I'm not—" Ethan started, then stopped. "Okay, yeah. I'm terrified."

"Good," Ramos said. "Terrified means you'll be careful. Means you'll pay attention. It's the guys who aren't scared who get people killed." He finished his coffee. "Look, counselor, nobody expects you to be an operator on day one. Hell, nobody expects you to be an operator ever. That's not your job. But we do expect you to be professional, to learn fast, and to not be a liability. Can you do that?"

"Yes."

"Then you'll be fine." Ramos stood. "Get some rest. Hydrate. We'll see you at the brief at 1400."

After they left, Ethan sat alone in the chow hall, staring at his half-eaten breakfast. Around him, contractors and soldiers ate and talked and laughed like this was just another day. Which, for them, it probably was.

For Ethan, it was the day he stopped being a lawyer and started being... what? A contractor? An observer? A participant in something he didn't fully understand?

He thought about Charleston, about his apartment near the law school, about the life he could be living—job interviews, bar association events, maybe dating that paralegal from the firm down the street.

Safe. Normal. Boring.

Instead, he was in Iraq. With a rifle he barely knew how to use and a job he didn't fully understand and a team that was probably wondering why MVM had sent them a would-be lawyer fresh out of school instead of someone with actual experience.

Public service takes many forms.

Ethan hoped this was the right form. He hoped he wouldn't screw it up. He hoped he'd survive long enough to figure out what he was doing.

He finished his coffee—terrible, but caffeinated—and headed back to his CHU to try to rest before the 1400 brief.

Sleep didn't come. He lay on his cot, staring at the metal ceiling, listening to the sounds of the FOB: generators humming, vehicles moving, the occasional distant thump that might have been controlled detonation or might have been something worse.

This was real. He was actually here. And tonight, he'd go outside the wire for the first time.

Ready or not.

The briefing room was packed. Twenty guys, maybe more, all in various stages of kit—some in full body armor, some in just t-shirts and cargo pants. Maps covered the walls. A satellite image was projected on a screen at the front.

Ethan slipped into the back, trying to be invisible.

"All right, listen up," the briefing officer—a Army captain with a ranger tab—started clicking through slides. "We've got SIGINT indicating high-value target is using this compound as a meeting site. Vehicle surveillance confirms unusual traffic patterns. We're going to hit it tonight, 0200 local."

The slides showed the target compound from multiple angles. Ethan tried to follow along, taking notes on the pad he'd brought. The military terminology washed over him—"egress routes," "CCP," "CASEVAC," "rules of engagement." He knew some of it from his training, but hearing it in context, in preparation for an actual mission, was overwhelming.

"Legal?" The captain looked right at Ethan. "You following this?"

"Yes, sir," Ethan lied.

"Good. Because if we detain anyone, I need you to verify we're doing it by the book. New administration's already talking about increased oversight. I don't want any congressional inquiries because someone forgot to read a detainee his rights or whatever the hell the bureaucrats are worried about this week."

Some guys laughed. Ethan felt his face flush.

After the brief, Ramos found him. "You get all that?"

"Most of it."

"Bullshit. But that's okay. Here's what you need to know: We're going to drive to the target compound. We're going to surround it. We're going to breach the door and clear the building. If we find bad guys, we'll detain them. Your job is to watch and make sure we do the detainee handling correctly. That's it."

"What if something goes wrong?"

"Like what?"

"Like... I don't know. What if we get shot at?"

Ramos's expression was unreadable. "Then you stay down, don't get in the way, and let us handle it. This is our job, counselor. We're good at it. You just focus on yours."

The pre-mission staging area was controlled chaos. Guys checking weapons, loading magazines, adjusting gear. The energy was different from the briefing—less casual, more focused. Game faces going on.

Ethan fumbled with his body armor, trying to remember how the damn thing was supposed to fit. Kozlowski noticed and came over.

"Here. Sides first, then shoulder straps." He adjusted the vest. "Not too tight—you need to be able to breathe. And make sure your magazines are accessible. You probably won't need them, but if you do, you'll want to be able to reach them."

"Thanks."

"First time's always weird," Kozlowski said, loading rounds into a magazine with practiced efficiency. "You'll get used to it."

"Does it stop being scary?"

"No. You just get better at dealing with scared." He slapped a full magazine into his rifle, charged the weapon. "But hey, bright side—statistically, most missions are boring as hell. We'll probably hit the compound, find nothing, and be back here by 0400 drinking bad coffee and wondering why the intel's always wrong."

"And if it's not boring?"

Kozlowski met his eyes. "Then you'll find out what you're made of."

The MRAPs were massive, imposing vehicles that looked like something from a science fiction movie. Ethan climbed into the back of one, wedging himself between Ramos and another contractor named Torres. The interior smelled like sweat and gun oil and fear.

"Comms check," Ramos said, and everyone tested their radios—a cacophony of voices calling out numbers.

"Reaper-6, clear."

"Reaper-2, clear."

"Reaper-4, clear."

Ethan's radio squawked. He fumbled with it. "Uh, Reaper... Legal? Clear?"

Torres grinned. "We're gonna need to work on your callsign, counselor."

"All elements, prepare to roll," a voice crackled over the radio.

The MRAP's engine rumbled to life. The ramp closed with a heavy clang that made Ethan's stomach lurch. This was it. They were actually doing this.

"Nervous?" Ramos asked.

"Yeah."

"Good. Keeps you alert." He checked his rifle one more time. "Remember—stay close, do what I say, and you'll be fine."

The MRAP lurched forward, and through the small window, Ethan watched the FOB's lights recede into darkness. They were outside the wire now. Outside the relative safety of the base. In Indian Country, as some of the guys called it.

In the real Iraq.

The ride was maybe twenty minutes, but it felt like hours. Every bump, every turn, every shadow outside the window could be an IED, an ambush, a rocket. Ethan's hand kept drifting to his rifle, checking the safety, making sure it was still there.

"Relax, counselor," Torres said. "You're gonna give yourself a heart attack before we even get there."

"How are you all so calm?"

"We're not," Ramos said. "We're just better at hiding it."

The convoy slowed. Stopped. The ramp dropped, and Iraqi heat poured in like a living thing.

"Move out," someone said, and they were flowing out of the MRAP, weapons up, spreading out in the darkness.

Ethan followed Ramos, trying to remember everything from training. Stay low. Watch your spacing. Don't silhouette yourself. His body armor felt heavier than before. His rifle felt too big in his hands. His heart hammered against his ribs.

Through his night vision goggles—issued that afternoon, barely tested—the world was green and grainy. The target compound was ahead, a low building surrounded by a wall. Figures were moving into position. Hand signals he half-understood.

Everything was happening so fast.

A breaching charge detonated—louder than anything Ethan had ever heard, even through his ear protection. The door blew inward. The team flowed through like water.

"GET DOWN! GET DOWN! HANDS!"

Ethan stayed outside with Ramos, watching the entry team do their work. Inside the compound: shouting, movement, the controlled chaos of professionals doing what they'd trained for.

"Clear!"

"Clear!"

"We got two MAMs, no weapons visible!"

Ethan's job now. He followed Ramos inside, where two Iraqi men sat on the floor, hands zip-tied behind their backs, looking terrified. An interpreter—not someone Ethan had met yet—was speaking to them in rapid Arabic.

"Counselor," Ramos said. "You're up. Make sure we're doing this right."

Ethan pulled out his notepad with shaking hands and started checking the procedures he'd memorized: detainees secured properly, not injured, treated with basic dignity. Biometric data being collected. Personal effects catalogued. An interrogator asking questions through the interpreter, not threatening, not coercive.

It was all textbook. All legal. All by the book.

And somehow, watching these two terrified men sitting on the floor of their own home while American soldiers stood over them with rifles, it felt wrong anyway.

"Counselor?" Ramos prompted. "We good?"

Ethan looked at his notes. Everything checked out. Everything was legal.

"Yeah," he said. "We're good."

The ride back to the FOB was quieter. The two detainees sat hooded in the MRAP, breathing heavily but not struggling. The operation had taken maybe forty-five minutes start to finish. Clean. Professional. No shots fired.

Boring, just like Kozlowski had predicted.

So why did Ethan feel like he'd just participated in something he didn't fully understand?

Back at the FOB, the debriefing was quick. The detainees were handed over to the detention facility. The intel guys were already analyzing phones and documents seized from the compound. The team was securing their weapons and gear, the post-mission routine as practiced as the mission itself.

"Good work, counselor," Ramos said, clapping him on the shoulder. "You did fine."

"I didn't do anything."

"You did your job. Observed, documented, verified we were following procedures. That's what we needed." He paused. "First mission's always strange. Don't overthink it. Get some rest. We'll do it again tomorrow."

Tomorrow. Of course. This wasn't a one-time thing. This was the job. Night after night, operation after operation, for the next six months.

Ethan walked back to his CHU through the pre-dawn darkness. The FOB was quiet, most people asleep or just waking for the day shift. Somewhere in the distance, he heard helicopters taking off.

In his CHU, he dropped his gear in a pile and sat on his cot. His hands were shaking—delayed adrenaline dump, probably. His body armor had left red marks on his shoulders. His feet hurt from the weight of all the gear.

He looked at his rifle, propped against the desk. He'd carried it for hours. Hadn't fired it. Probably wouldn't fire it tonight or tomorrow or any time soon.

But he'd carried it into Iraq. Into a combat zone. Into a situation where, if things had gone differently, he might have needed to use it.

That was real. That had actually happened.

His laptop was still on his desk. He opened it, found the WiFi signal, pulled up a blank document. Started typing.

Day 1. First mission. Target compound outside Baqubah. Two detainees, no resistance. Everything by the book. Don't know how to feel about it.

He stopped. Deleted it. Some things you couldn't write down. Some things you just had to carry.

He thought about Sterling's words: *Public service takes many forms.*

He thought about his mother's email: *Be safe.*

He thought about the two Iraqi men sitting on their floor, hands zip-tied, while Americans searched their home.

He thought about Ramos saying, *We're good at it.*

And he thought about tomorrow night, when they'd do it all over again.

Welcome to Iraq.

Welcome to the war.

Welcome to whatever the hell he'd just signed up for.

Ethan lay back on his cot and stared at the metal ceiling of his CHU. The AC wheezed. The generators hummed. Outside, the FOB was waking up to another day.

He'd survived his first mission. That was something.

Now he just had to survive the next one. And the one after that. And all the ones that would come between now and February, when his contract would end and he could go home and take the bar exam and pretend none of this had happened.

Except he knew, even then, that he'd never really be able to pretend. That something had changed tonight. That the version of him who'd stepped off that C-130 this morning was already someone different from the version lying here now.

He'd crossed a line. Entered a world. Become part of something he didn't fully understand but couldn't walk away from.

Not yet.

Not for six more months.

Sleep came eventually, fitful and fragmentary, full of green-tinted images and the sound of breaching charges and the faces of two terrified men who'd probably done nothing wrong except live in the wrong place at the wrong time.

When he woke a few hours later to the heat and noise of an Iraqi afternoon, Ethan Caldwell realized something:

He wasn't a lawyer anymore. Not really.

He was something else now.

He just didn't know what yet.

Three Weeks Later

Ethan had been on seven operations. Some boring, some tense, all exhausting. He'd learned to sleep through helicopter noise and distant explosions. He'd learned which body armor adjustments prevented the worst shoulder pain. He'd learned to eat the DFAC food without tasting it. He'd learned a dozen things they never taught in law school.

And he'd learned that Ramos was right—you didn't stop being scared. You just got better at dealing with it.

Tonight was supposed to be another standard operation. A courier moving money through a market in Baghdad. Snatch-and-grab. Easy.

What Ethan didn't know—couldn't know—was that tonight would be different. Tonight, a man with a fake limp would pull a Makarov pistol. Tonight, Ethan would spot the threat before anyone else saw it. Tonight, he would stop being the new guy and start being part of the team.

But that was still hours away.

For now, he just prepared his kit, checked his rifle, and tried to ignore the fear that never quite went away.

Just another mission.

Just another night.

Just Iraq.

4

THE MARKET

E than Caldwell had been warned about New Baghdad's markets. Crowded, chaotic, a pickpocket's paradise—and a perfect spot for an IED to turn a Tuesday into a memorial service. But the intel was hot: a low-level AQI courier was moving cash through the Shorja Market, linking facilitators to bomb-makers. The mission was a snatch-and-grab—take the courier, secure the cash, get out before anyone noticed.

"Stay close, counselor," Ramos said as they rolled out at 0900. "Market's a zoo. Don't get lost."

The team—Ramos, Kozlowski, Torres, and a new SEAL named Hayes who looked about nineteen—was dressed civilian: cargo pants, loose shirts over body armor, ball caps to blend in. Ethan's M4 was slung low under a jacket, his keffiyeh more for concealment than style. The market was a half-hour drive from the FOB, in a beat-up Toyota Land Cruiser that looked like every other car in Baghdad.

"Ever been to a souk?" Torres asked, chewing gum like he was on a road trip, not a raid.

"Charleston has a market," Ethan said.

Torres snorted. "Yeah, this is like that, except with more AKs and less artisanal cheese."

"Plenty of actual goats though," Hayes added.

"Jesus, not the goats again," Kozlowski muttered from the front seat.

The Shorja Market hit them like a wave—spices, grilled meat, and sweat mingling with the honk of scooters and shouts of vendors hawking everything from knockoff Nikes to live chickens. Stalls lined narrow alleys, tarps blocking the sun, bodies pressed so close Ethan could smell yesterday's garlic on the guy next to him. The team spread out, keeping visual contact, radios crackling in their ears.

"Target's in a blue dishdasha, red scarf," Ramos murmured over the comms. "SIGINT has his phone pinging near the spice stalls. Move slow, eyes sharp."

Ethan's job was straightforward: shadow the team, watch for complications, make sure the grab went clean. Three months into his rotation, he'd done enough of these to know the rhythm—positive ID, quick extraction, minimal scene. His contractor instincts just wanted to get home without a bomb going off.

They weaved through the crowd, Kozlowski's bulk parting bodies like a ship through waves. Ethan stayed a step behind, cataloging details: a kid selling cigarettes, a woman haggling over tomatoes, a guy with a limp who kept glancing their way.

Something about the limping man caught Ethan's attention. The limp looked too pronounced, almost theatrical. And his eyes—they weren't watching the crowd, they were tracking the team.

"There," Hayes whispered, nodding toward a man in a blue dishdasha, red scarf tied loose. He was buying cardamom, counting cash from a plastic bag. Ethan caught the glint of a phone in his hand—same model as the SIGINT hit.

"Confirm visual," Ramos said. "Torres, Hayes, flank left. Koz, with me. Counselor, cover the exit."

Ethan moved to a stall selling pistachios, pretending to browse while keeping the courier in his periphery. The team closed in like sharks—smooth, deliberate. Ramos bumped the courier "accidentally," checking for weapons. None visible. Torres slipped behind, ready to grab.

The limping man moved.

He was fast—way too fast—the limp vanishing as he pulled a Makarov pistol from under his jacket, bringing it up toward Ramos's back.

Ethan's instincts kicked in before thought. "Gun!" he shouted, his hand already moving toward his M4.

The crowd froze for a half-second, then scattered like startled birds. The man fired—*crack-crack*—missing Ramos but hitting a stall, wood splintering. Ramos spun and dropped, tackling the courier to the ground. Kozlowski's M4 came up in one fluid motion, three-round burst, precise. The gunman collapsed.

"Move! Move!" Ramos yelled, zip-tying the courier's wrists as the man shouted in Arabic. Hayes and Torres formed up, weapons raised, scanning for additional threats.

The market was pandemonium. Vendors diving behind stalls. Shoppers running in every direction. A donkey somewhere braying in distress. Ethan backed toward their exit alley, M4 up, heart hammering but hands steady, scanning for more shooters.

"Vehicle, now!" Kozlowski bellowed, dragging the courier to his feet. The plastic bag of cash had split open, dinars scattering across the ground like confetti.

"Grab what you can!" Ramos ordered.

Ethan snatched bills off the ground, stuffing them into his jacket pockets—evidence, not theft. They were sprinting now, the courier half-running, half-being-carried between Hayes and Torres.

Gunfire cracked behind them—more shooters, though Ethan couldn't tell if they were AQI or just armed shop owners who thought they were being robbed. Torres pivoted, fired a controlled burst back down the alley. "Contact rear!"

"Keep moving!" Ramos shouted.

The Land Cruiser was where they'd left it, engine running, driver—a contractor named Phillips—scanning with barely controlled panic. Hayes shoved the courier into the back seat, face-first. Ethan dove in last, someone's boot catching him in the ribs as the door slammed.

"Go! Go! Go!"

Phillips floored it, the SUV lurching into Baghdad traffic with a squeal of tires. Horns blared. A scooter swerved to avoid them. Behind them, the market receded into a haze of dust and lingering chaos.

"Headcount!" Ramos barked.

"All present!" Kozlowski confirmed, already checking his magazines. "Counselor, you hit?"

Ethan checked himself—ribs sore where he'd been kicked, adrenaline making his hands shake slightly, but no blood. "I'm good."

The courier was babbling in Arabic, face-down across the backseat. Hayes zip-tied his ankles for good measure. "Shut the fuck up," he said, not unkindly, then looked at Ethan. "Good call on the gunman, counselor. That was a clean spot."

"Saved Ramos's ass," Torres added from the front seat.

"Just doing my job," Ethan said, trying to keep his voice steady. His mouth was dry. The adrenaline was starting to convert into something else—not fear, exactly, but a delayed understanding of how close that had been.

Ramos was on the radio: "Reaper-6, package secure, one hostile KIA, exfiling to base, no friendlies injured."

"Copy, Reaper-6," the TOC crackled back. "QRF on standby if needed."

"Negative on QRF. We're clear."

The drive back was tense but uneventful, just the hum of the engine and the courier's muffled protests against the seat cushion. Ethan clutched the wad of dinars he'd grabbed—evidence now, part of the case they'd build against the network. His mind kept replaying the sequence: the gunman's fake limp, the weapon coming up, his own shout, Kozlowski's shots, the way the body had dropped.

He'd spotted the threat. Called it out. Ramos was alive because of him.

That should feel good, right?

It did. Sort of. Mostly it just felt loud in his head.

Back at the FOB, they processed the courier through the standard routine—biometrics, photographs, initial interrogation by specialists who spoke fluent Arabic and knew which questions to ask. The salvaged cash went to the intelligence cell for analysis—serial numbers, forensic traces, anything that could map the financial network.

"Good haul," a major from the fusion cell said, flipping through the bills. "This'll help us trace their funding sources. And the phone's a gold mine—contacts, call logs, maybe texts if he wasn't smart about OPSEC."

Ethan nodded, still processing. He retreated to his CHU and started his report:

Operation conducted IAW applicable ROE. Target positively identified via SIGINT correlation and visual confirmation. Hostile actor engaged team with deadly force, presenting imminent threat to team members. Hostile neutralized per established protocols. Target secured without injury. Estimated 15-20 civilian bystanders present during engagement; no civilian casualties reported. Detainee handled consistent with applicable directives. Evidence secured and transferred to appropriate personnel.

Assessment: Lawful action under AUMF and applicable ROE. Successful capture operation.

Clean. Professional. The kind of report that would survive review.

He leaned back, feeling the adrenaline crash starting to hit—that hollow, shaky feeling that came after. There was a knock on his door. Kozlowski poked his head in, tossing him a warm Red Bull from someone's care package stash.

"You called that gunman before any of us saw him," Kozlowski said. "Good eyes, counselor."

"Just lucky," Ethan said, cracking the can. The sweet, chemical taste was somehow exactly what he needed.

"Luck's part of it. But you were paying attention. That's what matters." Kozlowski paused in the doorway. "Ramos wanted me to tell you—that was solid work today. You're not just the legal guy anymore. You're one of us."

After Kozlowski left, Ethan sat in the quiet of his CHU, letting that sink in. *One of us.* He'd crossed some threshold he hadn't even known existed—from observer to participant, from the guy taking notes to part of the team.

He thought about Charleston, about the bar exam waiting for him in February, about the life he was supposed to be building. About the careful planning that had led him to this: a plywood room in Iraq, still smelling of gunpowder, processing the fact that he'd helped save lives today by spotting a threat before it could kill.

Not him pulling the trigger—that was Kozlowski's job. But Ethan had seen the pattern. Made the call. Set it in motion.

The distinction mattered. For now.

That night, lying in his bunk, Ethan couldn't sleep. The market kept replaying in his head—not the violence, but the moment before it. The pattern he'd noticed. The man with the fake limp who'd been watching them. The way his body had moved when he went for the gun, too fluid, like the limp had been an act all along.

He'd seen it. Processed it. Called it.

Saved Ramos.

The rotation would continue. More missions. More compounds. More moments like this where everything could go wrong but didn't because someone was paying attention.

He was starting to understand what this job actually was. Not the analysis he'd thought he'd be doing back at Harvard. Not the detached legal observer role he'd imagined. This was something else—a kind of presence, a constant alertness, reading situations and people and danger in real time.

And apparently, he was good at it.

Two weeks from now, he'd be stateside for a training cycle. After that, back here. More markets, more raids, more chances to prove he belonged.

But tonight, in his CHU at FOB Warhorse, Ethan Caldwell was just a 25-year-old contractor trying to figure out who he was becoming.

The adrenaline was fading now, leaving behind something simpler. Not regret. Not pride exactly. Just recognition that he'd done the job, done it well, and the team was intact because of it.

Tomorrow there'd be another mission. Another compound. Another briefing.

But tonight, he'd take the win.

Sleep came eventually, fitful and fragmentary, full of crowds and gunfire and the smell of cardamom.

5

CONTACT

T he op was supposed to be simple: observe and report.

A farmhouse three klicks west of the city, suspected meeting site for AQI leadership. No raid tonight—just eyes on, see who shows up, capture imagery, build the pattern of life. Tomorrow night, maybe the night after, they'd come back with a bigger element and kick the door.

Tonight was just Ethan and four operators: Ramos, Kozlowski, a Green Beret named McKnight, and Torres from SEAL Team 5. Light and quiet. In at dusk, out before dawn.

"Remember, counselor," Ramos had said during the brief, "we're ghosts tonight. Nobody knows we're here, nobody sees us, we go home for breakfast. Easy day."

Ethan should have known better. Two weeks after the market, he'd learned that nothing in Iraq was ever easy.

They'd inserted two hours after sunset, dropped off by a pair of MRAPs that immediately rolled back toward the FOB. The farmhouse sat in the middle of cultivated fields—grain, maybe, or something that had been grain before the drought. A single dirt road connected it to the main highway. One story, flat roof, typical Iraqi construction. Lights on inside.

The team set up in a drainage culvert two hundred meters out, the kind of concrete tube that channeled irrigation water during the growing season but now just provided concealment. Through his NODs, Ethan could see the house clearly—one vehicle parked outside, a beat-up Opel, no guards visible.

"Too quiet," McKnight whispered. He was the oldest of the group, maybe thirty-five, with the weathered look of someone who'd done multiple rotations. "Don't like it."

"It's a farmhouse, not a fortress," Torres said. "What'd you expect, guard towers?"

"I expect *something*. Dogs. Kids. Somebody smoking on the roof."

"Maybe they're all inside watching TV," Kozlowski suggested.

"Iraqis don't watch TV at 2100," McKnight said. "They're outside. Always outside. This feels wrong."

Ramos keyed his radio, spoke quietly to someone back at the TOC. Listened. Keyed again. "TOC confirms—SIGINT still shows activity at this location. Target phone is here. We sit tight, observe."

So they sat. Watched. Waited.

Ethan's job was to document everything—who came, who left, what time, what vehicles. Later, the intel guys would correlate it with signals intercepts and drone footage and build a target package. But that was future work. Right now he just had to stay awake, stay quiet, and try to ignore the smell of the culvert, which suggested it hadn't been entirely dry when they'd climbed in.

At 2145, headlights appeared on the dirt road.

"We got movement," Ramos said softly. "Two vehicles. Toyota pickup and... looks like a sedan. Can't tell the make."

The vehicles pulled up to the farmhouse. Men got out—Ethan counted six, maybe seven in the darkness. Military-age males, some carrying what looked like AKs. They went inside. The lights stayed on.

"Bingo," Torres whispered. "Meeting."

Kozlowski had a camera with a telephoto lens, snapping photos. The shutter sound seemed impossibly loud in the silence, but Ethan knew it couldn't carry two hundred meters. Still, every click made him flinch.

Another thirty minutes passed. Then another vehicle—this time a larger truck, maybe a Hilux. More men. The house was getting crowded.

"How many you count?" Ramos asked.

"Twelve, maybe fifteen," McKnight said. "Plus whoever was already inside."

"That's a lot for a meeting."

"Or a wedding," Kozlowski said. "Remember that wedding we almost hit in Ramadi?"

"This isn't a wedding," Ramos said. But he radioed the TOC anyway, relaying the numbers.

Ethan kept taking notes, logging times and vehicles. His handwriting was terrible in the dark even with a red-lens flashlight, but that was a future problem. He'd transcribe it later, clean it up, add it to the intelligence file that would eventually justify—or not justify—a raid.

At 2230, the door of the farmhouse opened and someone stepped out. Through his NODs, Ethan watched a man walk about twenty meters from the house, stop, look around.

Then look directly at their culvert.

"Shit," McKnight breathed. "He's looking right at us."

"He can't see us," Ramos said. "We're two hundred meters out, no light signature, no movement."

But the man kept staring. Then he pulled out a phone, made a call, spoke for maybe thirty seconds. Put the phone away. Went back inside.

"That's not good," Torres said.

"Could be nothing," Ramos said, but his voice had changed. Tighter. "Could be calling his wife."

"At 2230?" McKnight said. "After staring at exactly where we are? Come on."

Ramos was already on the radio. "TOC, Reaper-6. Possible compromise. Request immediate exfil."

The response crackled back: "Reaper-6, TOC. Nearest QRF is twenty mikes out. Can you hold?"

Twenty minutes. Ethan felt his heart rate kick up. Twenty minutes was forever.

"Reaper-6 copies," Ramos said. "Standing by."

They waited. The house stayed lit. No one came out. But Ethan couldn't shake the feeling that something had changed. The air felt different. Heavier.

At 2245, the door opened again and men started pouring out. Not casually—quickly, purposefully. They went to the vehicles, opened trunks, started pulling out weapons. Not just AKs—Ethan saw what looked like a PKM machine gun, maybe an RPG.

"Contact imminent," Ramos said into the radio, voice still calm but urgent. "We are gonna need that QRF right fucking now."

"They're flanking," McKnight said, watching through his optic. "Left and right. Classic L-shaped ambush. They know exactly where we are."

"How?" Torres demanded.

"Doesn't matter," Ramos snapped. "Koz, you got the 240?"

Kozlowski was already shifting, pulling the M240 machine gun into position. "Yeah."

"McKnight, Torres, right side security. Counselor—"

"Stay down, don't get shot, I know the drill," Ethan said, trying to keep his voice steady.

The men from the farmhouse had spread out into the darkness, moving through the fields in fire teams. Professional. Coordinated. These weren't farmers. These were fighters.

"TOC, Reaper-6," Ramos said, and now there was genuine urgency in his voice. "We are about to be in a very bad spot. Where is my QRF?"

"Fifteen mikes," came the response. "Hold what you got."

"Tell them to hurry the fuck—"

The first rounds snapped over their heads before he finished the sentence.

The sound of an AK on full auto is distinctive—a sharp, rapid *crack-crack-crack* that sounds nothing like the movies. The rounds hit the berm above the culvert, throwing dirt and rocks. Ethan pressed himself into the concrete, his heart hammering so hard he thought it might crack a rib.

"Contact right!" McKnight yelled, and returned fire—controlled bursts from his M4, the muzzle flash bright even through NODs.

More fire from the left. Kozlowski opened up with the 240, the heavier gun making a deeper sound: *thud-thud-thud-thud-thud*. Sustained bursts, tracer rounds arcing out into the darkness like malevolent fireflies.

"RPG!" someone yelled—Ethan didn't catch who—and then there was a *whoosh* and an explosion thirty meters to their right. The shockwave hit like a physical thing, compression and heat and noise all at once.

"We gotta move!" Torres shouted. "They got our position!"

"Where the fuck are we gonna move to?" McKnight shot back, firing another burst. "It's open ground for two hundred meters!"

Ramos was on the radio, voice clipped and professional even as rounds cracked overhead: "TOC, Reaper-6, troops in contact, taking fire from multiple positions, we need CAS, we need QRF, we need something right fucking now!"

Another RPG, closer this time. Ethan felt the heat wash over the culvert. His ears were ringing. The smell of cordite and burning vegetation filled the air.

Kozlowski was still hammering away with the 240, sweeping left to right. "They're trying to flank!" he yelled. "Got shooters moving through the field!"

"Light 'em up!" Ramos ordered, and pulled a flare from his kit. Popped it. The red phosphorous burned bright, casting everything in hellish crimson. Ethan could see them now—figures moving through the grain, at least a dozen, maybe more.

Too many. Way too many.

Torres threw a grenade—the M67 tumbled through the air, detonated with a sharp crack. Someone screamed in the darkness. But the firing didn't stop.

"Counselor!" Ramos grabbed Ethan's shoulder. "You got your rifle?"

"Yeah—"

"Then use it! Anything that moves out there is trying to kill us!"

Ethan had qualified with the M4. Had done the training at the range. But he'd never fired at a human being. Never wanted to. In the market he'd spotted the threat, but Kozlowski had pulled the trigger. Now there was no Kozlowski between him and the decision.

A man appeared in the grain field, fifty meters out, raising an AK.

Ethan's body moved before his brain caught up—muscle memory from training, adrenaline, pure survival instinct. He brought the M4 to his shoulder, put the EOTech red dot on center mass, squeezed the trigger.

The rifle bucked. Once. Twice. Three times.

The figure dropped.

Ethan stared, frozen, the rifle still at his shoulder. He'd done it. Put rounds into a human being and watched him fall.

"Good shot, counselor!" McKnight yelled. "Keep firing!"

There were more of them. So many more. Ethan fired again, didn't know if he hit anything. The world had contracted to the red dot sight, the crack of rounds overhead, the sound of his own breathing loud in his ears. His hands were working independently of his thoughts—acquire target, fire, acquire target, fire.

Kozlowski's 240 went silent. "Changing barrel!" he shouted, and Torres shifted to cover his sector, rifle barking in rapid semi-auto.

"Reaper-6, TOC," the radio crackled. "QRF is inbound your pos, five mikes, and we have fast movers overhead in ten. Can you mark your position?"

"IR strobe!" Ramos yelled, and McKnight pulled out an infrared strobe light—invisible to the naked eye but bright as the sun through NODs or aircraft sensors. He set it up on the berm, the team's lifeline to salvation.

Another RPG. This one hit the culvert's edge, the explosion deafening. Ethan felt something hot slash across his left arm, looked down, saw his sleeve torn and blood welling up. Not a lot. Shrapnel, maybe. Or a rock fragment.

It burned, but the adrenaline was too high for pain. He kept firing.

"They're pulling back!" Torres shouted. "Vehicles are moving!"

Through the chaos, Ethan could see it—the Hilux and the pickup truck peeling away from the farmhouse, headlights on now, racing toward the highway. The fighters in the field were collapsing back, providing covering fire as they withdrew.

They'd heard the radio traffic. Knew the QRF was coming. Knew they were about to get hit from the air.

The firing slackened. Became sporadic. Then stopped entirely.

The silence was almost worse than the noise.

The QRF arrived in a thunder of MRAPs and Strykers, dismounts flooding into the field. An Apache helicopter roared overhead, searching for fleeing vehicles. But the fighters were gone—vanished into the warren of roads and villages that made pursuit impossible without starting a full-scale operation.

A medic looked at Ethan's arm, cut away the torn sleeve. "You're fine," he said, cleaning the wound. "Shrapnel, looks like. Couple stitches when we get back, you'll have a nice scar to show off."

"Great," Ethan muttered.

They swept the farmhouse. Found blood trails. Shell casings. Two bodies in the field—one was the man Ethan had shot, lying in the grain with three holes in his chest. An AK beside him. A phone in his pocket. The other was farther out, victim of Kozlowski's 240.

"Intel's gonna want those phones," someone said.

Ethan stared at the body—*his* body, the man he'd killed. The guy looked young. Couldn't have been more than twenty-five. Someone's son. Maybe someone's father. Wedding ring on his finger.

Dead because Ethan had put three rounds in him.

"Hey." Ramos was beside him. "You did good, counselor. That was a clean shoot. He was about to light us up. You saved lives tonight."

"Yeah," Ethan said.

"I mean it. No hesitation. Right call. That's what this job is."

"Yeah."

They loaded up and rolled back to the FOB as dawn broke over Diyala Province. Ethan sat in the MRAP, his arm throbbing now as the adrenaline faded, his ears still ringing, the smell of gunpowder clinging to his clothes.

McKnight offered him a bottle of water. "First time?"

"First time what?"

"First time in a real firefight. First time shooting someone. First time knowing for sure you killed somebody."

Ethan took the water, drank. His throat was raw. "Yeah."

"Gets easier," McKnight said. Then, after a pause: "Actually, that's bullshit. It doesn't get easier. You just get better at dealing with it."

"Great," Ethan said.

"Look at it this way—you went to Iraq, got in a gunfight, killed a bad guy, and you're going home with a cool scar. That's more than most people can say."

"Most people don't have to," Ethan said quietly.

McKnight nodded. "True. But you're not most people anymore. You're one of us now. For real this time."

Back at the FOB, there was a debrief. Ethan walked through what happened, gave his statement, handed over his notes. The intel guys were ecstatic—the phones from the dead fighters had contacts, messages, everything they needed to map the network.

"Outstanding work," a major told Ramos. "Real operator shit out there."

Ramos just nodded, tired.

The medic stitched up Ethan's arm in the aid station—seven stitches, neat and professional. "Keep it clean, change the dressing daily, it'll scar but not too bad. You got lucky."

In his CHU, Ethan stripped off his body armor and looked at the bandaged arm. The white gauze was already showing a small spot of blood seeping through. It would scar. A permanent reminder.

He thought about the man in the field. Wondered who he'd been. What brought him to that farmhouse. Whether he'd known what he was getting into or if he'd just been in the wrong place at the wrong time. Whether his wife—if that's what the ring meant—would ever know what happened to him.

Then he thought about Ramos and McKnight and Kozlowski and Torres, about how close they'd come to dying in that culvert. About how the QRF had arrived with five minutes to spare and what would have happened if they'd been ten minutes out instead.

He'd killed a man tonight.

Saved his team.

Both things were true.

Both things would always be true.

Ethan lay down on his bunk, closed his eyes, and tried to reconcile that.

He was still trying when sleep finally came.

Two days later, his arm stitched and bandaged, his report filed, Ethan was on a rotator back to Charleston. He sat in the red light of the C-17's cargo bay, surrounded by Marines and soldiers rotating home, and touched the bandage on his arm.

It would leave a scar. A permanent reminder of the night he stopped being an observer and became a participant. The night he killed someone. The night the line between analysis and action disappeared completely.

He wondered if that was what he'd always been headed toward, and just hadn't wanted to admit it.

The plane banked west, toward home, toward two weeks of decompression before the next training cycle.

Ethan closed his eyes and tried to sleep.

All he saw was the red dot sight, center mass, the figure dropping in the grain.

He didn't sleep much on the flight home.

But when he did, he dreamed of markets and gunmen and patterns in the chaos, and somewhere in those dreams was the understanding that he'd found something he was good at, even if it cost more than he'd expected.

6

THE POINT

E than adjusted the bandage on his left arm as Petey's F-150 rumbled through the pine forests of eastern North Carolina. The stitches were still fresh—just over a week old—and the wound itched like hell under the gauze.

"You should get that looked at when we're there," Petey said, nodding at the arm. "They've got a solid med facility."

"Medic at Warhorse said it's fine. Just needs to heal."

"Yeah, but Harvey Point's got the good stuff. Might as well take advantage."

They'd been driving for two hours since leaving Virginia Beach, getting deeper into the kind of rural North Carolina that consisted of pine trees, more pine trees, and the occasional gas station. Ethan had spent the last week stateside, decompressing from the Baqubah firefight, trying not to think about the man in the grain field every time he closed his eyes.

"Ramos vouched for you after the market thing in Baghdad," Petey said. "You spotted that gunman before any of us did. Then you held your own in that firefight outside Baqubah—kept your head, put rounds downrange when it mattered. That's what got you the invite to Harvey Point."

"I shot someone," Ethan said quietly.

"Yeah, you did. And we all went home because of it." Petey glanced over. "Look, I don't know what's going on in your head right now. First time you kill somebody, it fucks with you. That's normal. But you did the job. Clean shoot, no hesitation when it counted. That's what we're gonna sharpen at The Point—make sure next time feels less like chaos and more like execution."

"Is that supposed to be reassuring?"

"It's supposed to be honest."

Harvey Point Defense Testing Activity sat on a peninsula jutting into the Albemarle Sound, surrounded by water on three sides and fences on the fourth. The gate had no sign, just a guard shack with two very serious men who checked IDs with the kind of thoroughness that suggested they'd done this before.

"Peterson and Caldwell," Petey said, handing over their CAC cards. "We're on the roster for the three-day."

The guard checked a list, made a phone call, checked the list again. Finally nodded. "Pull up to the admin building. Someone will meet you."

They drove through a landscape that looked deceptively peaceful—woods, some buildings that could have been warehouses or barracks, what appeared to be a water tower. Then they rounded a corner and Ethan saw it: a mockup village that looked like it had been transported directly from Iraq or Afghanistan. Mud-brick walls, narrow alleys, the whole thing.

"Holy shit," Ethan said.

"Yeah," Petey said. "They've got multiple mockups. Middle East, Central Asia, even some Eastern European stuff. Plus ranges, kill houses, a maritime training area—the whole nine yards."

"Who else is here?"

"Your team, mostly. Ramos, Kozlowski, Torres, McKnight, Hayes. Some other guys from the task force. We do this every rotation—keep skills sharp, try out new techniques, blow shit up in a controlled environment instead of doing it for real."

A man in his forties with a weathered face and the standard contractor look—5.11 pants, polo shirt, wraparound sunglasses—met them at the admin building.

"Peterson, good to see you again. This the guy from Baghdad?"

"Ethan Caldwell," Ethan said, shaking hands.

"Mike Brennan. I run training here. Heard about the market op and the firefight in Baqubah. Ramos says you've got good instincts." His eyes dropped to Ethan's bandaged arm. "That from Baqubah?"

"Shrapnel. It's fine."

"Get it checked by our medics anyway. Last thing we need is an infection taking you out during training." Brennan looked back at his face. "You ever done formal CQB training? Kill house work?"

"Some, in contractor orientation. Nothing like this."

"Then you're in for an education. Drop your gear in Building 3, range orientation starts in thirty minutes."

The orientation was given by a former Delta operator named Davis who spoke in the clipped, efficient manner of someone who'd briefed thousands of operations and had no patience for stupid questions.

"Harvey Point is a training facility operated by CIA's Special Activities Center," he said, standing in front of a whiteboard. "Everything you see here, everything you do here, everything you learn here is classified. We train personnel in advanced tactical skills, demolitions, maritime operations, and close-quarters battle. The ranges are hot, the training is realistic, and if you do something stupid, you will get hurt. Questions?"

Hayes raised his hand. "Is it true you guys blew up a 747 here once?"

"No comment. Other questions?"

"What's the deal with the mockup village?" Torres asked.

"We've got three full-scale training environments," Davis said, clicking to a slide that showed an overhead map. "Middle Eastern village, Central Asian compound, and what we call 'Generic Bad Guy Hideout' which works for pretty much anywhere. You'll be rotating through all three over the next three days. We'll start with CQB refreshers, move to demolitions tomorrow, and finish with integrated scenarios on day three."

Ramos leaned over to Ethan. "Translation: today we shoot things, tomorrow we blow things up, day three we shoot things that we blow up."

"Living the dream," Ethan muttered, absently touching his bandaged arm.

The first day was kill house work—running through the mockup structures in fire teams, clearing rooms, engaging pop-up targets. Ethan had done some of this in contractor training, but Harvey Point took it to another level. The targets were sophisticated—some innocent, some hostile, some ambiguous. The scenarios were complex. And the instructors were absolutely merciless.

"CIVILIAN!" an instructor yelled after Ethan shot a target that turned out to be holding a cell phone, not a gun. "That's a kid with a phone! Congratulations, you just created an international incident!"

"The lighting was bad!" Ethan protested.

"The lighting's always bad! That's why it's called combat! Run it again!"

By lunch, Ethan's arms were sore from holding his rifle up, his ears were ringing despite the hearing protection, and he'd been "killed" by pop-up targets at least six times. His left arm throbbed where the stitches pulled.

"You're doing fine," McKnight said, handing him a bottle of water. "Everyone sucks the first few runs. It's muscle memory—you gotta build it."

"I feel like I should be better at this. I've been in actual firefights."

"Real firefights are different. This is training—you're thinking too much. In Baqubah you just reacted. Here you're trying to apply what you learned, but you haven't internalized it yet." McKnight drained his own water. "Give it time. By day three you'll be running through these houses without thinking."

The afternoon was more of the same, but Ethan started to find his rhythm. Stop thinking, start moving. Trust the instincts. When a target popped up, shoot or don't shoot based on what you saw, not deliberation. By the end of the day, he'd only gotten "killed" twice and hadn't shot any civilians.

"Progress," Ramos said during the debrief. "Tomorrow we learn to make things go boom. How's the arm holding up?"

Ethan glanced at the bandage, now slightly dingy from sweat and dust. "It's fine. Itches more than anything."

"Get it re-dressed tonight. Last thing we need is you getting an infection."

Day two started with a classroom session on demolitions—types of explosives, placement techniques, fusing systems, safety protocols. The instructor was a soft-spoken former Special Forces engineer who treated C-4 with the casual familiarity most people reserved for lunch meat.

"This is a basic breaching charge," he said, holding up what looked like a small brick of clay. "You can shape it, mold it, stick it to surfaces. It's stable—you can shoot it, drop it, set it on fire, and it won't detonate. But add a blasting cap with an electrical charge..." He smiled. "Then it gets interesting."

They spent the morning learning to build charges—door charges, wall charges, vehicle charges. Ethan's hands learned the work quickly: measure, cut, shape, place detonator, run det cord. His left arm protested occasionally when he had to put weight on it, but the medic had re-dressed it that morning and declared it healing well.

The afternoon was practical application: blowing up cars in a designated demolition range.

"We've got some donated vehicles from the junkyard," the instructor explained, gesturing to a field containing half a dozen beat-up sedans. "Your job is to render them inoperable using minimum explosives. Think of it as terrorist vehicle interdiction—you want to disable the car, not vaporize the neighborhood."

Ethan's team went third. They placed charges on the engine block, the fuel tank (empty, thankfully), and the transmission. Ran det cord. Set up the firing device. Everyone retreated to a bunker two hundred meters away.

"This is your show, counselor," Ramos said, handing Ethan the firing device—a simple box with a key and a trigger.

Ethan looked at the device, then at the car sitting in the field. He turned the key. "Fire in the hole!"

Squeezed the trigger.

The car didn't explode so much as *disassemble*—the hood blew straight up, spinning lazily in the air before crashing down fifty meters away. The transmission dropped out the bottom. Windows shattered. The fuel tank deformed but didn't rupture. When the smoke cleared, what remained was definitely never driving again.

"YEAH!" Torres yelled, slapping Ethan on the back—carefully avoiding the injured arm. "Counselor just smoked that Civic!"

"That was a Corolla," Hayes said.

"Whatever! It's dead now!"

Even Ethan couldn't help grinning. There was something primal and satisfying about making things explode in a controlled environment. For a moment, the memory of the man in the grain field receded.

"Good placement," the instructor said, reviewing the footage. "Clean detonation, effective damage, no fragmentation outside the safe zone. That's exactly what you want. Now do it four more times until it's muscle memory."

They spent the rest of the afternoon systematically destroying vehicles. By the time they finished, Ethan could build a door charge blindfolded and calculate blast radius in his head. His hands smelled like C-4—a weird, almost sweet chemical smell that wouldn't wash out easily.

"Tomorrow's the fun day," Petey said at dinner—actual hot food in a small cafeteria, though everyone still called it the DFAC out of habit. "Integrated scenarios. You'll use everything you learned."

"Define 'fun,'" Ethan said.

"The kind of fun where we shoot things and blow things up simultaneously."

"That does sound fun," Ethan admitted.

Day three started at 0400 with a brief that felt more like a real mission than a training exercise.

"Intelligence indicates a high-value target is operating out of a compound in the Middle Eastern mockup village," Davis said, showing satellite photos that looked eerily real. "Your team will conduct a capture/kill operation. Target is potentially armed, may have guards, structural integrity of the buildings is unknown. You'll need to breach, clear, and secure. This is a live-fire exercise with role players acting as hostile forces using simunitions. They will shoot back. Questions?"

"Rules of engagement?" Ramos asked.

"Same as downrange. Positive ID before engaging. Watch for civilians—we've got role players mixed in. Treat this like a real op."

They geared up in full kit—body armor, helmets, NVGs, live ammunition for breaching charges but simunitions for actual shooting. Ethan checked his rifle three times, made sure his demo kit was properly packed, tried to channel the adrenaline into focus. His arm still ached, but it was manageable.

"You good, counselor?" McKnight asked, noticing him adjusting the bandage under his sleeve.

"Yeah. Ready."

"Good. Stay sharp. This is as close to real as it gets without actual bullets."

The mockup village was even more convincing at 0500 in the pre-dawn darkness—narrow alleys, compound walls, the distant sound of a call to prayer playing over loudspeakers to add atmosphere. They moved in on foot, clearing corners, checking rooflines.

A figure appeared in a doorway. Ethan's finger found the trigger—but then he saw the figure was holding a broom, not a weapon. Civilian. He didn't fire.

The figure nodded and disappeared back inside.

"Good discipline," Ramos whispered. "Just like Baqubah—read the situation first."

They reached the target compound. McKnight and Ethan placed breaching charges on the door while the rest of the team stacked up. The charges were real—this was live demo, not simulation. Ethan's hands were steady as he ran the det cord, muscle memory from yesterday's training.

"Breacher ready," Ethan reported.

"On my count," Ramos said. "Three... two... one... execute."

Ethan squeezed the trigger. The charges detonated with a crack that rattled his teeth, the door blowing inward. The team flowed through the breach, weapons up.

Inside was chaos—role players with simunition weapons, pop-up targets, civilian role players trying to flee. Ethan shot a hostile who appeared from behind a curtain, the simunition round marking his chest. Moved to the next room. Another hostile, engaged. A civilian cowering in the corner—didn't engage.

His body was moving on instinct now, the chaos of Baqubah translated into controlled aggression. Target identification, fire discipline, room clearing—it was all flowing together.

"Stairs!" Torres called, and they moved up to the second floor.

The "target" was in the back room—a role player with his hands up, looking appropriately terrified. They zip-tied him, secured the building, called it in.

"Objective secure," Ramos reported. "One EKIA, target captured, two civilians secured."

They extracted back through the village, the scenario ending as they reached the extraction point where a vehicle waited.

Davis was there with a clipboard, taking notes. "Time from breach to capture: four minutes, thirty seconds. Acceptable. No civilian casualties. Good fire discipline. Ethan—" He looked at Ethan. "You hesitated on the first room entry. Why?"

"Checking for civilians."

"Good. But you need to move faster while checking. In a real op, that hesitation could get you killed. Run it again."

They ran it three more times that morning, each iteration slightly different—different target locations, different role players, different complications. By the third run, Ethan's time from breach to capture was under four minutes and he wasn't hesitating anymore. His injured arm was screaming at him, but he pushed through it.

The afternoon was a maritime scenario—small boat insertion to a waterfront compound, basically everything they'd learned applied to a dock complex. Ethan had never done small boat ops before, and he spent most of the approach trying not to fall out of the Zodiac as it bounced across the Albemarle Sound.

"This is awful!" he yelled over the engine noise.

"This is awesome!" Hayes yelled back, grinning like a maniac.

The raid went smoothly—they came in from the water side, breached a boathouse, secured the mock compound. Ethan only fell in the water once, and only because Torres "accidentally" pushed him during the extraction. At least the cold water felt good on his throbbing arm.

By 1600, they were done. Three days, dozens of scenarios, hundreds of rounds fired, and more explosions than Ethan could count.

The final debrief was surprisingly brief.

"You all did good work," Davis said. "Ethan, you kept up with operators who've been doing this for years. That's not nothing. The Baqubah firefight obviously taught you some things—you've got the basics of staying calm under fire. We just refined it. Ramos, your team's CQB times are competitive with any SMU—keep that sharp. Everyone: remember that training is perishable. Use it or lose it. See you next rotation."

Driving back to Virginia Beach in Petey's truck, Ethan felt simultaneously exhausted and energized. His body hurt in new and interesting ways. His ears were still ringing. His left arm was definitely going to need fresh bandages and probably another medical check when he got back. He smelled like gun smoke and C-4 and swamp water.

"So," Petey said, "what'd you think of The Point?"

"I think I get why you guys don't talk about it much," Ethan said. "Because 'I spent three days learning to blow up cars and raid mockup villages' sounds insane when you say it out loud."

"Wait till you try explaining it to civilians."

"I'm not explaining it to anyone. My family thinks I'm doing international trade consulting."

"Right. Very consulting. Much trade." Petey grinned. "You did good out there, counselor. Davis doesn't usually compliment people. If he says you kept up, that means something. And you worked through that arm injury without complaining—that counts too."

"Thanks." Ethan watched the pine forests roll past.

"After Harvey Point, you're gonna be a real asset to the team. No more 'just the legal guy'—you're a shooter now. Trained, qualified, proven."

They drove in comfortable silence for a while, watching the landscape change from deep pine forest to slightly less deep pine forest.

"Can I ask you something?" Ethan said.

"Shoot."

"How long you been doing this? The contracting work."

"Since 2005. Did four years active duty, got out, realized I missed it. Went contractor. Better pay, more flexibility, pretty much the same work." Petey glanced over. "Why?"

"Just wondering. Trying to figure out what the career path looks like."

"Career path," Petey laughed. "Counselor, there's no career path. You do it till you don't. Till you get hurt, or tired, or meet someone who makes you want to stop. Or till the contracts dry up. There's no pension plan for kicking doors."

"Reassuring."

"It's honest." Petey turned on the radio, found a country station. "But you're different. You got the law degree. You got options most of us don't. You can always go be a lawyer if this doesn't work out."

"Yeah," Ethan said, "I guess I can."

But even as he said it, he wondered if that was still true. If you could go back to being a lawyer after you'd killed someone. After you'd learned to breach doors and blow up cars and clear rooms full of hostiles. After you'd found something you were good at, even if it cost pieces of yourself you hadn't known you had to give.

Two weeks later, Ethan was back on a rotator to Iraq, his demo skills fresh, his CQB times faster, and his rifle work smoother than it had ever been.

Harvey Point had been intense, exhausting, and—if he was being honest—transformative. Three days that turned him from someone who'd survived combat into someone who could excel at it.

The bar exam was still months away. Iraq was right now.

And after Harvey Point, he felt ready for whatever came next.

Even if he still saw the man from the grain field every time he closed his eyes.

7

THE DITCH

T he night vision goggles turned the world into a grainy green hellscape. Ethan Caldwell moved in a low crouch behind Staff Sergeant Ramos, his boots whispering through the dust of what had once been someone's front yard. His left arm still had the pink scar from Baqubah—healed now, but a permanent reminder. Somewhere ahead, beyond the maze of mud-brick compounds and collapsed walls, was a house where a mid-level AQI facilitator supposedly slept.

Or didn't. Intelligence was like that—50/50 on a good day.

"Hold," came the whisper through the radio. The line of operators froze.

Ethan pressed himself against a wall, feeling the retained heat of the day radiating through his body armor. His role tonight was observation—watch the detainee handling, make sure nobody violated the guidelines. Four months into this rotation now, and he'd learned that "military-age male" could mean a seventy-year-old farmer, and that the lines between analyst, observer, and participant had all but disappeared.

The Harvey Point training had helped. He moved more confidently now, his body remembering the patterns even when his mind was elsewhere.

The village—he didn't know its name, doubted it had one that appeared on any map—was silent except for the occasional bark of a dog in the distance. These settlements outside Baqubah all looked the same: clusters of single-story homes connected by narrow alleys and irrigation ditches, the kind of place where insurgents could vanish like smoke.

"Terp up," Ramos whispered.

Yousef materialized from the shadows, thirty-something, former Baghdad University literature professor turned interpreter because American dollars spent better than Iraqi dinars. He wore the same kit as the operators—body armor, helmet, rifle—but Ethan knew the calculus was different for him. Get caught by AQI, and Yousef's death would make the evening news for its creativity.

"Tell him we need to know which house," Ramos said, nodding toward an old man who'd emerged from a doorway, hands already raised.

Yousef started forward, crossing the narrow alley between compounds.

He never saw the ditch.

One moment he was moving with the careful economy of someone who'd done fifty of these missions. The next, he simply *disappeared* with a wet splash and a strangled yelp that was almost—but not quite—swallowed by the noise discipline everyone maintained.

The smell hit them two seconds later.

"Oh, *Jesus*," someone hissed through the comms.

Ethan bit down on his tongue to keep from laughing. This was serious. They were on an operation. People could die.

But Christ, the *smell*.

Yousef emerged from the drainage ditch like a swamp creature from one of those horror movies, sewage dripping from his helmet, his body armor, his rifle. The ditch—maybe three feet deep and two feet wide—carried the runoff from a dozen houses. In rural Iraq, that meant everything: dishwater, waste, things Ethan didn't want to contemplate.

"I'm okay," Yousef whispered in English, then added something in Arabic that Ethan's limited vocabulary suggested was considerably more profane.

Ramos made a hand signal: *continue mission*.

They moved forward, but now Ethan could track Yousef's position by smell alone. It was like someone had weaponized a backed-up septic tank. In the confines of the narrow alleys, there was no escaping it.

The old man they needed to question took one look at Yousef, wrinkled his nose, and started talking immediately. No translation needed—he just pointed at a house and unleashed a stream of Arabic that sounded a lot like "take what you want, just get that smell away from me."

The target house was empty. The facilitator had moved—bad intelligence, or good tradecraft, or just the normal friction of war. They zip-tied the old man anyway (gently, by the book), photographed him for the database, and extracted back to the vehicles.

In the MRAP, Yousef sat alone in the very back, as far from everyone else as physics allowed.

"Man," said Torres, one of the team's junior operators, "I think something died in here."

"Yeah," said Ramos, deadpan. "Yousef's dignity."

"Fuck you," Yousef said, but he was smiling. Ethan could see it even in the red glow of the interior lights.

"Seriously, though," said Mitchell, the team medic, "we're gonna need to hose you down before you get back on the FOB. Like, with industrial chemicals. Maybe fire."

"Napalm," suggested Torres. "It's the only way to be sure."

"I hate all of you," Yousef said.

"No you don't," Ramos said. "You love us. We're the only people in Iraq who'll stand downwind of you."

"Not anymore we won't," Mitchell added.

Even Ethan joined in. "I'm pretty sure there's something in the Geneva Conventions about chemical weapons, Yousef. We might have to file a report."

"Oh, *now* you care about the Conventions," Ramos said, grinning.

The laughter rolled through the MRAP, the kind that came from too much adrenaline and too little sleep and the strange intimacy of people who'd just walked through darkness together and come out the other side. Yousef took it all with the grace of someone who knew that this—the ribbing, the abuse, the belonging—was the price of admission.

Ethan found himself laughing harder than he had in weeks. Since before Baqubah. Since before the man in the grain field. The absurdity of it was almost therapeutic—a reminder that not everything in Iraq was life and death, that sometimes it was just sewage and bad luck and the kind of humor that came from shared misery.

Back at the FOB, they did hose him down. With actual hoses. In his gear. Yousef stood in the shower trailer for forty-five minutes while the rest of the team convened outside like it was a tailgate party.

"Think his rifle still works?" Torres asked.

"Rifle's fine," said Mitchell. "It's been through worse. Unlike Yousef's reputation."

Someone—Ethan never found out who—had already made a sign for Yousef's bunk: "SWAMP THING SLEEPS HERE."

Later, after the debrief and the paperwork and the empty feeling that came from another dry hole, Ethan sat in his CHU and tried to write something coherent in his journal. The words wouldn't come. How did you explain that you'd spent the night watching a literature professor crawl through sewage so that American operators could kick down doors looking for ghosts? How did you capture the strange alchemy that turned horror into humor, fear into friendship?

He settled for: *Yousef fell in a ditch. Smell was unbelievable. Mission unsuccessful but everyone came home.*

From the next CHU over, he could hear Ramos's voice: "Hey Yousef, tomorrow we're hitting another village. Try to stay topside, yeah?"

And Yousef's reply: "Tomorrow I'm calling in sick. You all can drown in ditches yourselves."

The laughter that followed sounded like the only sane thing in a country that had forgotten what sanity looked like.

Three days later, Ethan was back in Charleston, walking through the humidity of a Lowcountry November, trying to remember why he'd thought this life made sense. In two weeks he'd be back on a rotator, flying east again, back to the ditches and the darkness and the men who turned sewage into stories.

His bar exam study materials sat unopened on his kitchen counter. February felt both very close and impossibly far away.

He'd get to them. Eventually.

Right now, he just wanted to sleep in a bed that didn't smell like Yousef. And maybe, for a few hours, not think about the man in the grain field or the fact that he was becoming someone he didn't entirely recognize.

But the laughter from the MRAP stayed with him. That, at least, felt real. Human. A reminder that even in the darkness, there were moments of light.

He'd take it.

8

THE MEDEVAC

The operation wasn't theirs.

Ethan sat in the TOC at 0230, nursing terrible coffee and watching the tactical display track another team's mission three klicks north. His team—Ramos, Kozlowski, Torres, McKnight—sat around the plywood room in various states of boredom. They were on standby, the backup element, which meant sitting in full kit watching other people work.

"Reaper-4, TOC," the radio crackled. Different callsign. Different team.

"Go ahead."

"We've got one urgent surgical. IED strike, one friendly WIA. Requesting immediate CASEVAC."

The room changed. Everyone sat up straighter. The bored energy vanished.

"Nature of injuries?" the TOC officer asked, already pulling up the medevac grid.

"Shrapnel, lower extremities and abdomen. He's conscious but losing blood. We need a bird now."

Ramos was already standing, keying his radio. "TOC, Reaper-6. We're two klicks south of their position. We can roll for emergency extraction if the bird's delayed."

The TOC officer looked at the map, did the math. The medevac helicopter was fifteen minutes out. Reaper-4's position was exposed—they'd need to move the casualty to a better landing zone. Ramos's team could be there in eight minutes.

"Reaper-6, TOC. You're authorized to move. Coordinate with Reaper-4 for linkup."

"Copy. Reaper-6 moving."

Ethan grabbed his rifle—reflex now, after three months. His Harvey Point training kicked in: check magazine, chamber round, safety on. He followed the team out to the MRAPs, his heart rate already elevated.

This wasn't the plan. This wasn't their op. But someone was bleeding.

The ride was fast, the MRAPs pushing through the darkness at speeds that felt reckless. Ramos was on the radio coordinating with Reaper-4, getting grid coordinates, casualty status updates.

"Counselor," Kozlowski said from across the MRAP. "You ever done a CASEVAC before?"

"No."

"Stay out of the way. Let the medics work. Your job is to watch our perimeter while they stabilize him."

Ethan nodded. His mouth was dry. This wasn't like the firefights—those had been abstract, targets at distance, figures in night vision. This was going to be blood and screaming and someone from their side dying.

They rolled up to Reaper-4's position seven minutes later. The other team had moved the casualty to a clearing, a small patch of dirt road where the medevac could land. In the green glow of Ethan's NODs, he could see them: five operators in a defensive perimeter, and in the center, two men bent over a body on the ground.

Ramos's element deployed fast. McKnight and Torres took up security positions. Kozlowski moved straight to the casualty with their medic—a contractor named Wilson who'd been a Special Forces 18D, the real deal.

Ethan followed, his rifle up, scanning the darkness. Stay out of the way. Watch the perimeter.

But he couldn't help looking.

The wounded operator—a SEAL from Team 5, maybe twenty-four years old—lay on his back in the dirt. His pants were shredded below the knee. Even through the NODs, Ethan could see the dark stain spreading across the ground. Too much blood. Way too much blood.

The kid was conscious. That was somehow worse. His face was pale, visible even in the green darkness, and he kept trying to sit up.

"Stay down, brother," Wilson said, his voice calm but firm. He was cutting away the remains of the SEAL's pants, exposing the damage. "You're gonna be fine. Bird's inbound."

"My legs," the SEAL said. His voice was surprisingly steady. "Can't feel my legs."

"That's the shock. Don't worry about it. Just breathe."

Wilson worked with practiced efficiency: tourniquet on the thigh, pressure dressing on the abdomen where more shrapnel had hit. His hands were covered in blood within seconds, but they didn't shake.

Ethan stood five meters away, rifle up, ostensibly watching the perimeter. But he couldn't stop glancing back. The SEAL's teammate—another young guy, maybe the same age—was kneeling beside him, holding his hand.

"You're good, man. You're good. Bird's coming."

"Tell my mom—"

"Shut the fuck up. You're gonna tell her yourself. You're fine."

The medevac helicopter appeared over the horizon, running lights off, just the sound of rotors cutting through the night. The downwash kicked up dust as it settled onto the road, and the crew chief jumped out with a litter.

Wilson gave the handoff brief—quick, professional, medical terminology that Ethan barely followed. The SEAL was loaded onto the litter, and four operators carried him to the bird. His teammate climbed in with him, still holding his hand.

Thirty seconds later, the helicopter lifted off, banked west toward the combat support hospital, and disappeared into the darkness.

The silence after was strange. Too quiet. Just the sound of generators from a distant compound and the wind through the palms.

Ethan realized his hands were shaking.

Ramos appeared beside him. "You good?"

"Yeah."

"First time seeing it up close?"

Ethan nodded.

"He gonna make it?"

"Probably. Wilson got the tourniquets on fast. Blood loss looked bad but he was still conscious, still talking. That's a good sign." Ramos keyed his radio. "All elements, prepare to exfil."

The ride back was quiet at first. Ethan sat in the MRAP, his rifle across his lap, trying to process what he'd just seen. The blood. The kid's face. His teammate holding his hand.

"Counselor's awful quiet," Torres said after a few minutes. "You gonna throw up?"

"No."

"First CASEVAC always fucks with you," McKnight said. "I puked after mine. Ramadi, 2006. Guy took an RPG, lost both legs. Made it to the bird, died on the table."

"Jesus," Ethan muttered.

"This one's gonna make it though," Kozlowski said. "Wilson knows his shit. Kid'll be drinking beer in Germany in a week, telling everyone how he got blown up."

"Better story than falling in a ditch," Torres added.

"Or getting chased by a goat," McKnight said.

Even Ethan smiled at that. "Hayes is never living that down."

"Never," Kozlowski agreed. "Forty years from now, he'll be at some SEAL reunion, and someone's gonna bring up the goat."

"Good," Torres said. "Builds character."

The humor was thin, forced, but it helped. The tension in Ethan's chest loosened slightly. This was how they processed it—dark jokes, references to absurdity, anything to push back against the weight of what they'd just seen.

Back at the FOB, the debrief was quick. The operations officer logged the incident—emergency CASEVAC, coordinates, timeline, casualty status at handoff. Clean. Professional. Just another line in the daily report.

"Good work out there," the TOC officer said. "Fast response, clean handoff. That's how it's supposed to work."

After they secured their gear, the team gathered outside the TOC. Nobody wanted to go straight to their CHUs. Nobody wanted to be alone with what they'd just seen.

"Chow hall's still open," Ramos said. "Who wants shitty eggs?"

"Always," Torres said.

They walked across the FOB in the pre-dawn darkness, still in full kit minus helmets. In the chow hall, they loaded trays and sat at their usual table in the back.

"Counselor did good," Wilson said, appearing with his own tray. His hands were scrubbed clean now, no trace of blood. "Kept his head, stayed out of the way. That's all I need."

"I didn't do anything," Ethan said.

"Exactly. You didn't panic, didn't need someone to babysit you. That's doing something." Wilson dumped ketchup on his eggs. "Kid's gonna be fine, by the way. Just got word from the CSH. Surgery went well. He'll keep the leg."

"Told you," Kozlowski said to Ethan. "Wilson knows his shit."

"Still gonna have a hell of a scar though," Wilson said. "Good one. Better than counselor's shrapnel scratch."

"It's not a scratch," Ethan protested, touching his left arm reflexively.

"Compared to tonight? It's a scratch." Wilson grinned. "But at least you got a good story. 'This one time, I got blown up in Iraq.'"

"Better than 'This one time, I fell in a ditch,'" Torres said.

"Or 'This one time, a goat chased me,'" McKnight added.

"We're never letting that go, are we?" Ethan asked.

"Never," Ramos confirmed.

They ate in comfortable silence for a while. The adrenaline was fading now, leaving behind exhaustion and something else—relief, maybe. The system had worked. The kid was alive. Twenty-three minutes from the call to surgery, and he was going to make it.

"You know what the real miracle is?" Torres said eventually. "We got through that whole thing without counselor needing to file a report about whether we followed proper medevac protocols."

"There are medevac protocols," Ethan said.

"And we followed all of them," Ramos said. "So no report needed. See? System works."

"This time," McKnight said.

"This time," Ramos agreed.

After breakfast, Ethan walked back to his CHU as the sun started to rise over Diyala Province. The FOB was waking up—soldiers heading to the gym, contractors starting their day shifts, the normal rhythm of life in a war zone.

He thought about the SEAL lying in a hospital bed in Germany right now, alive because Wilson had gotten tourniquets on fast enough. Because the helicopter had arrived in twenty-three minutes. Because the system had worked.

This time.

He thought about what Torres had said: *Better story than falling in a ditch.* That's how they did it—turned trauma into humor, horror into stories, fear into jokes about goats. It was how they survived. How they processed. How they kept going.

Ethan sat on his cot and looked at his hands. Clean now. No blood. Just like Wilson's.

His phone buzzed—an email from the TOC. *CASEVAC update: SSG Ramirez, Team 5, stable condition following surgery. Expected full recovery. Medevac response time: 23 minutes. Excellent work by QRF and medical personnel.*

Twenty-three minutes. The system had worked.

Ethan lay back and closed his eyes. He could still see the SEAL's face, pale in the green light. Could still hear his voice: *Can't feel my legs.* But he could also hear Torres making jokes about goats, McKnight ribbing him about his "scratch," Wilson saying *kid's gonna be fine.*

The membrane between observer and participant had been thin from the start. Tonight it had disappeared completely. He'd grabbed his rifle without thinking and rolled out to help someone he didn't know.

Not because of regulations or protocols or legal oversight.

Just because someone needed help.

That was the job. The real job. Not the analysis or the compliance monitoring or the reports. Just showing up when the call came and trusting that twenty-three minutes was enough.

This time, it had been.

Two weeks later, Ethan's team ran into Ramirez's teammate at the PX. The guy—a SEAL named Dixon—recognized them from the CASEVAC.

"Hey, you're the element that came out that night. The QRF."

"Yeah," Ramos said. "How's Ramirez doing?"

"Germany, then back to the States for recovery. He's gonna make it. Docs say he'll keep full mobility, might even stay in if he wants." Dixon paused. "Your medic—Wilson—tell him thanks. He saved Ramirez's life."

"Will do," Ramos said.

After Dixon left, Kozlowski looked at Ethan. "See? System worked. Kid's fine."

"Yeah," Ethan said. "This time."

"This time's all we got, counselor. This time's enough."

Ethan bought a Snickers and walked back across the FOB. The system had worked. Twenty-three minutes, and a kid got to go home instead of going in a box.

Slightly more good than harm.

That was the bar. That was all it could ever be.

And sometimes—just sometimes—that was enough.

9

TIJUANA

E than should have known better when Ramos suggested the long weekend. "Come on, counselor," he'd said at the team house outside Virginia Beach. "You've been shot at in Iraq, survived Harvey Point, and got that nice scar to prove it. But you've never been to TJ? That's backwards as hell."

So here he was: five of them packed into a rental SUV crossing the border at San Ysidro on a Friday afternoon. Besides Ramos, there was: Kozlowski, the quiet SEAL from Team 3 who could deadlift a Volkswagen; "Petey" Peterson, the former Green Beret now with SAD who'd been his guide at Harvey Point; Dockery, another SAD guy who'd done time with Delta; and Ethan, the only one without a trident or long tab, feeling like someone's kid brother tagging along.

"Legal's buying first round," Petey announced as they parked near Avenida Revolución. "Consider it payment for all those ROE briefings we don't listen to."

The strip was exactly what Ethan expected: neon signs, aggressive timeshare hawkers, Americans in tank tops stumbling between bars at 6 PM like it was last call. The air smelled like carne asada, exhaust, and bad decisions.

They hit a bar. Then another. Somewhere around the third, Kozlowski started a tab that would require a financial analyst to decode. The tequila in Tijuana didn't taste like tequila—it tasted like regret mixed with gasoline, but it got the job done.

"You good, counselor?" Ramos asked around 9 PM, when the street lights had come on and the real Tijuana started to wake up.

"I'm great," Ethan lied. He wasn't drunk—not quite—but he was loose enough that the edges of Iraq felt softer, farther away.

They were walking down a side street, looking for a taco stand Petey swore existed, when the guy appeared. Older Mexican man, maybe sixty, with the weathered face of someone who'd seen every kind of tourist.

"You boys want to see something *special*?" he said in perfect English. "Real Tijuana. Not this tourist shit."

"We're good, man," Dockery said, but Petey was already interested. "What kind of special?"

The man smiled. "A show. Very famous. You never forget."

"How much?"

"For you? Fifty American. Each."

Ramos looked at Ethan. "You ever been to a show in TJ?"

"I've never been to TJ at all until today."

"Then you *definitely* haven't lived." He turned to the man. "Lead the way, *jefe*."

They followed him through a doorway Ethan would have walked past without noticing—just a black door between a farmacia and a place selling knockoff soccer jerseys. Down a narrow hallway that smelled like cigarettes and desperation, then into a back room with maybe twenty other people, mostly men, mostly American, sitting in folding chairs around a small raised platform.

The lighting was dim. The walls were painted black. There was a woman on stage doing something with a beer bottle that defied physics and good judgment.

"Oh Jesus," Ethan muttered. "What is this place?"

"Culture," Petey said, grinning. "This is culture, counselor."

The beer bottle act ended to scattered applause. The woman left. There was a pause—too long, the kind that made Ethan wonder if this was where they got robbed—and then someone led an animal onto the stage.

A donkey.

"Oh no," Ethan said.

"Oh *yes*," said Kozlowski.

What happened next was... exactly what you'd expect at a legendary donkey show in Tijuana. Ethan's brain, trained at Harvard and Charleston Law, simply filed the whole thing under "inadmissible" and refused to process it further.

The crowd had mixed reactions. Some people cheered. Some looked horrified. Most looked like they couldn't decide which reaction was appropriate.

"This is the worst thing I've ever seen," Dockery said flatly. "And I saw a guy get hit by a VBIED in Ramadi."

"Can't unsee it," Ramos agreed. "That's going in the memory bank forever."

That's when Petey decided to document the moment.

He pulled out his phone—a beat-to-shit BlackBerry that had survived two deployments—and lined up a shot of the stage. Ethan saw him do it. Watched his thumb move toward the button. Wanted to say something.

The flash went off like a flashbang in the dark room.

CLICK-FLASH

Every head in the room turned toward them.

"Did you just—" Kozlowski started.

"¡TELÉFONO!" someone shouted in Spanish.

Two very large Mexican men who'd been lurking by the back wall suddenly looked very interested in their table.

"Oh shit," Petey said, which in Ethan's experience was never a good sign from a man who'd survived Tora Bora.

"Put it away," Ramos hissed. "Right now."

But it was too late. The men were moving toward them—not running, but walking with purpose. One of them was talking rapid-fire Spanish into a radio.

"We gotta go," Dockery said, standing. "Like, right now."

They stood as a unit—five Americans in a back room in Tijuana suddenly looking very sober and very tactical despite being in civilian clothes. The crowd scattered. The woman on stage grabbed the donkey's lead and hurried into the wings like this happened every weekend.

"*Señores*," one of the big men said, hand out. "The phone."

"I don't think so," Petey said, and Ethan watched him shift his weight in a way that suggested he'd done this dance before.

"Petey," Ramos said quietly. "Don't."

"The phone," the man repeated. "Or we have a problem."

The room had gone silent. Even the music had stopped. Ethan's heart was hammering. This was stupid. This was so incredibly stupid. They were about to start an international incident over a donkey show photo. After everything they'd survived in Iraq—the market, the firefight, the training—this was how it would end?

"How much?" Kozlowski said suddenly.

The man blinked. "What?"

"For the phone. How much?"

The man conferred with his partner in Spanish. "Two hundred. American."

"Done." Kozlowski pulled out his wallet, counted out bills, handed them over. "Keep the phone. Delete the picture. We never happened."

The tension in the room dropped like someone had opened a valve. The big man took the money, examined it, nodded.

"You leave now," he said. "Don't come back."

They didn't need to be told twice.

They were three blocks away, practically running, before anyone spoke.

"Two hundred dollars?" Petey said, incredulous. "That phone cost me forty bucks!"

"You almost started a firefight in a donkey show," Dockery said. "In *Mexico*. Do you know how that After-Action Report would read?"

"Forget the AAR," Ramos said. "Imagine explaining to the Agency why five contractors got arrested in TJ. 'Well sir, we were watching a woman have relations with livestock when Peterson here decided to practice his surveillance photography...'"

Even Ethan was laughing now, the adrenaline converting to something like hysteria. After Baqubah, after the man in the grain field, after everything—this absurd moment felt almost cleansing.

"I forgot about the flash," Petey said defensively. "Force of habit. You see something, you document it."

"Yeah, well, you documented us almost getting killed by cartel guys because you wanted a souvenir," Kozlowski said. "Next time, just buy a T-shirt like a normal person."

They made it back to the border crossing at 2 AM, sober from fear and the long walk. The CBP agent looked at their IDs, looked at their faces, and just shook his head.

"Donkey show?" he asked.

"How'd you know?" Ramos said.

"You got that look. See it every weekend." He stamped their passports. "Welcome home, gentlemen."

In the SUV heading back to San Diego, somewhere around 3 AM, Petey broke the silence.

"So we're never talking about this again, right?"

"Absolutely not," Ethan said.

"Never happened," Dockery agreed.

"What happens in TJ stays in TJ," Ramos added.

Kozlowski, driving, just grunted. "I want my two hundred bucks back."

"Bill it to Langley," Petey suggested. "Operational expense."

"Yeah," Ethan said. "I'm sure that'll go over great. 'Miscellaneous costs: donkey show bribe, two hundred dollars. Maintaining cover and avoiding international incident: priceless.'"

They laughed, but it was the tired kind, the kind that acknowledged they'd dodged something genuinely stupid. Ethan looked out the window at the lights of San Diego appearing in the distance.

He thought about how far he'd come from Charleston—from political science papers and law school seminars to firefights and now this. Fleeing a donkey show in Tijuana with a bunch of operators who treated the whole thing like a training exercise gone sideways.

The work in Iraq was real.

This? This was just absurd. And maybe that was exactly what he needed—a reminder that not everything had to be life and death, that there were still moments of pure, stupid humanity even in a life defined by violence.

Two weeks later, he'd be back in Iraq. Back to the serious work.

But for now, in the darkness of the SUV on I-5, he just closed his eyes and tried very hard not to think about donkeys.

He never went back to Tijuana.

Some lessons, he figured, you only needed to learn once.

10

— · —

THE GOAT

The mission brief mentioned a "rural compound with possible livestock." That should have been Ethan's warning.

They were hitting a suspected safehouse at 0300—standard capture operation, mid-level AQI facilitator, the usual drill. The target package showed a small farm complex: main house, a couple of outbuildings, some kind of animal enclosure. Intel said the target lived alone, which meant either the intel was wrong (likely) or they were about to have an easy night (unlikely).

"Probably goats," Ramos said during the brief, pointing at the satellite image. "See that pen? Every farm out here's got goats."

"I like goats," Torres said. "They're funny."

"You won't think they're funny when one of them starts bleating and wakes up the whole village," McKnight said. He was riding with them tonight, filling in for Kozlowski who'd caught some kind of stomach bug that had him confined to a bathroom.

"How loud can a goat be?" Ethan asked.

Everyone who'd been in Iraq longer than him just looked at each other and laughed.

"Counselor," Petey said, shaking his head, "you're about to learn something about goats."

They rolled out at 0200, four MRAPs carrying a dozen guys: SEALs, Green Berets, a couple of SAD contractors, and Ethan—no longer just the legal observer, not after the market, Baqubah, and Harvey Point. He was part of the team now, another shooter with a JD and a scar to prove he'd earned his place.

The farm was exactly where the satellite said it would be, about two klicks off the main road in the middle of absolutely nowhere. They dismounted half a klick out and moved in on foot through fields that smelled like fertilizer and regret.

The compound was dark. No lights, no movement, just the ambient sounds of rural Iraq at night: distant dogs, wind through palm trees, and—yes—the occasional bleat of a goat from somewhere in the darkness.

"Told you," Ramos whispered. "Goats."

They stacked up at the main house door. Breacher set the charge. Ethan stayed back with the command element, watching through his NODs as the team prepared to flow in. His demo training from Harvey Point made him appreciate the technical precision of the charge placement—just enough to blow the door, not enough to collapse the structure.

The breaching charge blew with its usual percussive authority, and the team flooded through the door. Ethan heard the familiar sounds: "GET DOWN! HANDS! SHOW ME YOUR HANDS!"

Then he heard something else: a sustained, terrified bleating that sounded less like a farm animal and more like a car alarm designed by Satan himself.

"What the fuck?" someone said over the radio.

"We got goats!" Torres yelled. "We got goats *inside* the house!"

"Inside?" Ramos said. "Why are there goats inside?"

"How should I know? They're just—JESUS, GET OFF ME!"

Through his NODs, Ethan watched a figure emerge from the house, running at full sprint. For a moment he thought it was the target fleeing—his hand went to his rifle, muscle memory from Baqubah. Then he realized it was Hayes, and he was being chased by what appeared to be the world's angriest goat.

"SHOOT IT!" Hayes yelled, looking back over his shoulder.

"I'M NOT SHOOTING A GOAT!" someone shouted back.

"IT'S TRYING TO KILL ME!"

The goat—a large male with impressive horns—was indeed making a determined effort to either gore Hayes or head-butt him into the next province. Hayes dodged left, then right, his rifle completely forgotten as he engaged in what could only be described as agricultural combat.

"Hayes, just kick it!" McKnight yelled, watching the spectacle with what Ethan recognized as the thousand-yard stare of a man who'd seen too much weird shit in Iraq.

"I'M TRYING! IT'S REALLY FAST!"

More goats were emerging from the house now—apparently the target had been keeping an entire herd in his living room. They scattered into the compound, bleating with the kind of volume that suggested they were very upset about the sudden home invasion and were determined to let everyone within three kilometers know about it.

"Clear the house!" Ramos ordered, trying to maintain some kind of operational discipline. "And someone help Hayes!"

Ethan watched Petey jog over to where Hayes was still playing matador with the aggressive male. Petey, who'd trained him at Harvey Point, who'd survived multiple tours in Afghanistan and ran Agency operations across three provinces, tried to shoo the goat away.

The goat charged him instead.

"OH COME ON!" Petey yelled, diving sideways. The goat missed him by inches, skidded in the dirt, turned around, and lined up for another pass.

"This is the worst op I've ever been on," Petey muttered, scrambling to his feet.

Inside the house, things weren't going much better. The target—a man in his forties wearing a dishdasha and looking absolutely bewildered—had been zip-tied and was sitting on the floor surrounded by at least six goats who seemed more interested in the operators than their owner.

"Why are there goats in your house?" Ramos asked through the interpreter.

The man looked at Ramos like he was an idiot. "It is winter," he said in Arabic. "The goats sleep inside when it is cold. Where else would they sleep?"

"Outside?" Ramos suggested. "In the goat pen? Like normal goats?"

"These are expensive goats," the man said with dignity, as if this explained everything.

One of the "expensive goats" chose that moment to start eating a map off the table—possibly important intelligence, possibly just a map, but definitely being consumed by a ruminant.

"GET THAT!" an intel sergeant yelled, lunging for the map. The goat, startled, bolted—with the map still in its mouth—and ran directly into Torres, knocking him into a wall.

"I HATE THIS COUNTRY!" Torres yelled, sliding down to sitting position.

Outside, Hayes and Petey had managed to corner the aggressive male goat in the animal pen, only to discover it wasn't alone. There were at least fifteen other goats in there, and their alpha male's distress had them all worked up into a frenzy of bleating and head-tossing.

"We should just leave," Hayes said. "Forget the whole op. Tell command we couldn't find the target."

"Target's already zip-tied inside," Petey pointed out.

"Then we put him back! We un-zip-tie him and leave and never speak of this again!"

"That's not how this works!"

"IT SHOULD BE!"

Ethan found himself laughing—actually laughing—for the first time since Tijuana. After everything he'd seen and done, this absurd chaos felt almost therapeutic. No bullets. No blood. Just goats and chaos and the kind of ridiculous moment that reminded you war wasn't always about life and death.

It took twenty minutes to get the situation under control. The target was loaded into an MRAP, still protesting that his goats needed to be fed in the morning and who was going to do that now? The aggressive male was finally contained in the pen. The goat with the map had been caught, the map recovered (mostly intact, if slightly damp with goat saliva), and the intelligence materials from the house had been secured.

"Headcount!" Ramos called. "Everyone here? Everyone got all their fingers? Nobody got gored by livestock?"

"Hayes almost died," Torres said helpfully.

"I did NOT almost die, I was TACTICALLY REPOSITIONING!" Hayes protested.

"You were running away from a goat."

"A LARGE goat. With horns. That's basically a battering ram with legs."

In the MRAP heading back to base, the target sat quietly between two operators, apparently having accepted his fate. The mood was less "successful combat operation" and more "embarrassed silence."

"So," Ethan said finally, "that happened."

"We don't talk about this," McKnight said firmly. "What happens with the goats stays with the goats."

"I'm filing a report," Ethan said. "It's my job."

"You write one word about goats in that report and I will personally ensure you get assigned to every single livestock-adjacent operation for the rest of your contract," Ramos threatened.

"How many livestock-adjacent operations could there possibly be?"

"You'd be surprised," Petey muttered darkly. "Afghanistan was all about the goats. And sheep. And one time, a very angry camel."

"I don't want to hear about the camel," Hayes said.

"Nobody wants to hear about the camel," Petey agreed.

Back at the FOB, they processed the target through the standard procedures. His house had yielded some useful intelligence—phone records, financial documents, and one map that bore suspicious teeth marks but was still readable. The detainee claimed he was just a farmer, but farmers didn't usually have detailed information about foreign fighter networks in their homes.

"Good operation," the major from the fusion cell said. "Clean capture, good intel haul."

"Thank you, sir," Ramos said, keeping a very straight face.

After the debrief, Ethan retreated to his CHU to write his report. He sat there for a long moment, fingers hovering over the keyboard, thinking about how to phrase this.

Operation conducted IAW applicable ROE. Target secured without injury. Intelligence materials recovered. Minor complications due to unexpected presence of livestock in primary structure. No impact on mission success.

That seemed professional enough. Vague enough. No one needed to know about Hayes running for his life or Torres getting knocked over or the map-eating incident.

There was a knock on his door. He opened it to find the entire team standing there: Ramos, McKnight, Torres, Hayes, Petey, and several others.

"We voted," Ramos said. "We're buying you a drink when we get back to Virginia Beach."

"For what?"

"For not putting 'Hayes got chased by a goat' in the official report," Hayes said.

"I haven't finished the report yet," Ethan pointed out.

"Yeah, but you're not going to. Because you're one of us now." Ramos clapped him on the shoulder. "And we take care of our own. Even if they occasionally get defeated by farm animals."

"I was NOT defeated—" Hayes started, but everyone just talked over him.

"Besides," Petey added, "wait till you hear about the camel story from Afghanistan. Then you'll understand why we don't discuss operations involving livestock."

"I really don't need to hear about the camel," Ethan said.

"Nobody does," McKnight agreed. "But you will. Eventually. Because that's what happens on long rotations. You hear all the stories you never wanted to hear."

Later that night, lying in his bunk, Ethan couldn't help but laugh. Three and a half years ago he'd been graduating from the College of Charleston, writing a senior thesis on soft power. Two years ago he'd been in law school, studying international law frameworks. Now he was in Iraq, writing sanitized reports about operations that involved both counterterrorism and angry goats.

His phone buzzed—an email from his mother back in Savannah, asking how he was doing, if his "consulting work" was going well, when he'd be home for Christmas.

He typed back: *Everything's fine. Work is interesting. Lots of unexpected challenges. Should be home for the holidays. Love you.*

He didn't mention the goats. Some things were too hard to explain.

From the CHU next door, he could hear Hayes and Torres still arguing.

"It was a tactical repositioning!"

"You literally screamed 'IT'S TRYING TO KILL ME' while running away!"

"That was a tactical assessment of the threat environment!"

"You're never living this down, Hayes. Never. When you're a crusty old SEAL telling war stories to your grandkids, someone's gonna bring up the goat."

Ethan smiled, closed his laptop, and tried to sleep. His mind drifted to Baqubah when he tried to sleep, of the man in the grain field. But tonight it didn't weigh as heavy. Tonight there was just the absurdity of goats and the laughter of men who'd survived worse.

Tomorrow they'd probably hit another compound. Maybe there'd be more goats. Maybe there wouldn't. Either way, he was starting to understand that war wasn't just firefights and intelligence analysis and moral complexity.

Sometimes it was just chaos and livestock and trying not to laugh when your teammate got chased by an angry farm animal.

He'd take it. It beat the alternative.

Outside, the generators hummed their eternal song, and somewhere in the distance, a dog barked at the Iraqi night.

No goats, though.

At least not until the next operation.

11

THE GOOD SHOOT

The brief was perfect. That should have been Ethan's first warning.

He sat in the plywood operations center at 2130 hours, watching Ramos lay out the mission on a satellite image tacked to the wall. Red circles marked compounds. Blue arrows showed approach routes. A grainy photograph of the target—Abu Khalil, mid-level facilitator for Al-Qaeda in Iraq—was pinned at the center like a wanted poster from the Old West.

"SIGINT puts him at this location," Ramos said, tapping the primary compound. "Three intercepts in the last forty-eight hours, all matching known patterns. Voice recognition confirmed. He's moving foreign fighters through Diyala Province, we take him tonight, we cut off a pipeline."

Ethan reviewed his notes. The intelligence package was solid—multiple sources, corroborating evidence. Abu Khalil was a legitimate military target. The compound was isolated enough to minimize civilian risk. The ROE was clear.

Five months into his rotation now, and this was the kind of operation that should go perfectly. Unlike the empty house after the ditch incident. Unlike the chaos with the goats. This was textbook.

"Legal's good," Ethan said.

Kozlowski looked up from checking his kit. He'd recovered from his stomach bug and was back to full strength. "Counselor says we're good, we're good. Let's roll."

They left the wire at 2300, four MRAPs carrying a mixed element: SEALs, Green Berets, Agency SAD guys, a couple of interrogators, and Ethan. The night was cool, almost pleasant, the kind of weather that made you forget that in four months this place would be a hundred and twenty degrees of misery.

Ethan rode in the second vehicle, wedged between Petey and Hayes. His Harvey Point training had made him more comfortable with the rhythm of these operations, but something about tonight felt different. Too smooth. Too certain.

"You ever done a perfect op?" Petey asked over the engine noise.

Ethan thought about it. The market had been close—until the gunman. Baqubah had been an ambush. Harvey Point was training. The ditch and the goats were... well, those were their own category.

"No," he said.

"Then you're about to see what it looks like when everything works. Intel's solid. Weather's good. Moon's up just enough. This is gonna be textbook."

"Don't jinx it," Hayes said, not looking up.

"I'm not superstitious."

"That's because you're an idiot," Hayes muttered.

They dismounted a kilometer from the objective and moved in on foot. Ethan's body knew the rhythm now—stay low, watch your spacing, don't silhouette yourself against the sky.

The compound appeared out of the darkness exactly where the satellite said it would be—a low-walled rectangular structure with a single entrance, palm trees providing cover, fields beyond. No lights.

No movement. Just the ambient sounds of rural Iraq: distant dogs, wind through the palms, the hum of insects.

Ramos hand-signaled the element into position. Breachers moved to the door. Snipers covered the angles. Ethan stayed back with the command element, watching through his NODs as the ballet unfolded.

The explosion of the breaching charge was shockingly loud even though Ethan expected it. Then the team was flowing through the door like water, voices shouting in Arabic and English: "GET DOWN! ON THE GROUND! HANDS! HANDS!"

Ethan waited. This was always the worst part—the seconds between entry and all-clear, when anything could happen.

Ramos's voice crackled through the radio: "Jackpot. We got him."

Inside the compound, the scene was almost anticlimactic. Abu Khalil sat on the floor, flex-cuffed, a black hood over his head. Three other military-age males were cuffed nearby—associates, probably, or maybe just unlucky houseguests. The operators had already cleared the rooms, documented everything with cameras, bagged evidence.

"Check this out," Dockery said, holding up a laptop. "Password protected, but we got phones too. Probably a treasure trove."

One of the intel guys was photographing documents spread across a table—handwritten notes, what looked like financial records, a map of Diyala Province with markings that meant nothing good.

"Counselor," Ramos said. "You're up."

This was Ethan's job: verify that the capture followed procedures, that evidence was being handled correctly, that detainee treatment met standards. He watched as the interrogators did their initial field screening—checking IDs, asking basic questions through an interpreter.

Abu Khalil—if that's who this really was—said nothing. Just sat there, hooded, breathing steadily. The guy was either well-trained or genuinely calm.

"Biometrics match," one of the intel sergeants confirmed, checking a handheld device against the target's fingerprints. "This is our guy. Ninety-eight percent confidence."

Ethan reviewed the detainee tags, the evidence logs, the photographs. Everything was correct. Not just legal—*perfect*. By-the-book. The kind of operation that would survive any inspector general review, any congressional inquiry, any front-page story in the Washington Post.

"We're good," Ethan said.

"Then let's exfil," Ramos said. "I want to be back for breakfast."

The ride back to the FOB was quiet. Abu Khalil sat in the back of Ethan's MRAP, hooded, hands cuffed behind his back, flanked by two operators who looked like they were guarding furniture. The detainee didn't struggle. Didn't speak. Just sat there as the vehicle bounced over the rutted roads.

Ethan watched him—or tried to. The hood made it impossible to see anything human. Just a shape. A target. A data point in the larger war.

"Good op," Petey said, breaking the silence. "Clean. No shots fired. Nobody hurt. Intel was spot-on. This is how it's supposed to work."

"Yeah," Ethan said.

"You don't sound convinced."

"I am. It was... it was perfect."

And it had been. That was the problem.

Back at the FOB, they processed Abu Khalil through the detention facility—more photographs, more biometrics, formal interrogation by specialists. Ethan observed, taking notes, making sure every regulation was followed. The detainee was given water. Offered food. Allowed to pray. Treated, by the standards of wartime detention, with dignity.

The evidence went to the intel fusion cell for analysis. The laptop would be cracked by specialists. The phones would yield contact networks, maybe intercepts. The documents would be translated and cross-referenced against other intelligence. Abu Khalil himself would be questioned, slowly, methodically, legally, until he either talked or didn't.

And then what? Ethan wondered. Trial? Indefinite detention? Transfer to Iraqi custody? There were procedures for all of it, frameworks, memoranda of understanding between governments. He'd read them all. Could cite chapter and verse.

But watching Abu Khalil sitting in a holding cell at 0600, still hooded, still silent, Ethan couldn't shake the feeling that something about this was wrong.

Not illegal wrong. Not immoral wrong.

Just... wrong.

He found Ramos in the chow hall at 0700, eating powdered eggs and drinking coffee that could strip paint.

"Hell of an op," Ramos said. "You write your report yet?"

"Working on it."

"Make us sound good. Command loves good news."

Ethan sat down with his own tray of barely edible breakfast. "Can I ask you something?"

"Shoot."

"How do you know we got the right guy?"

Ramos looked up, fork paused halfway to his mouth. "Biometrics matched. Intel was solid. You saw the evidence."

"Yeah, but... how do we *know*? Like, really know? The intercepts could be wrong. The voice recognition could be off. Maybe he's just a guy who sounds like Abu Khalil. Maybe—"

"Counselor," Ramos said, not unkindly. "You can't think like that. You'll drive yourself crazy. We had probable cause. Multiple sources. Corroborating evidence. That's the standard. That's all we can work with."

"But what if it's not enough?"

Ramos set down his fork. "Then we grabbed the wrong guy. And that sucks. But we followed the rules. Did our jobs. Made the best call with the information we had. That's all anyone can ask."

"Is it?"

"Has to be." Ramos picked up his coffee. "Look, you want certainty? You're in the wrong line of work. This isn't a courtroom. We don't get beyond reasonable doubt. We get 'best available intelligence' and 'military necessity' and we make calls. Sometimes we're right. Sometimes we're wrong. Tonight we were right. Take the win."

Ethan nodded, but something in his chest felt tight. He thought about the man in the grain field from Baqubah—the one he'd killed. At least there, the threat had been immediate. Visible. The guy had an AK and was shooting at them.

This was different. Quieter. More procedural. And somehow that made it worse.

He spent the rest of the day finishing his report. Typed it up on a ruggedized laptop in his CHU, laying out the facts with careful precision:

Mission conducted IAW applicable ROE and legal authorities. Target positively identified via biometric and SIGINT correlation. Detainee handled consistent with Geneva Conventions and applicable DOD directives. Evidence properly documented and secured. No civil-

ian casualties. No collateral damage. Assessment: Lawful detention of enemy combatant.

It was perfect. Clean. Unimpeachable.

He hit send and felt nothing.

That night—technically morning, 0200 again, the time when all missions seemed to happen—Ethan couldn't sleep. He lay in his bunk listening to the generators hum and thinking about Abu Khalil sitting in his cell. Was he sleeping? Praying? Wondering what happened to his life?

Or was he planning his next move? Figuring out how to beat the interrogators? Confident that his organization would continue without him?

Ethan didn't know. Couldn't know.

All he knew was that they'd done everything right, followed every rule, met every standard.

And somehow that made it worse.

Because if the perfect operation—the good shoot, the clean capture, the lawful detention—still left him feeling like this, what did that say about all the imperfect ones? The empty houses. The wrong guys. The collateral damage.

What did it say about the whole enterprise?

He touched his scar, feeling the raised tissue under his fingertips. That scar was from doing the right thing—protecting his team, stopping a threat. But it also marked the moment he'd killed someone. Both things were true.

Just like tonight. Perfect operation. Right guy. Clean capture.

And still something felt wrong.

Three days later, during his regular intel brief, Ethan learned that Abu Khalil had started talking. Gave up names, locations, plans. The laptop had yielded a network of foreign fighter facilitators across three provinces. The operation was being called a "significant intelligence success."

"See?" Petey said, slapping Ethan on the back. "Told you it was a good op."

"Yeah," Ethan said. "Good op."

His contract was up in six weeks. February bar exam was coming. Then Greenville, and the small law firm, and the quiet life he'd told himself he wanted.

But sitting in that briefing room, looking at the intelligence maps and target packages and success metrics, Ethan wondered if he could really walk away. If you could go back to estate planning after you'd done this. After you'd learned to be good at something that required pieces of yourself you'd never known existed.

The man in the grain field still haunted his dreams. But Abu Khalil would haunt him differently—not because the operation went wrong, but because it went perfectly right.

And Ethan was starting to understand that sometimes the perfect operations were the hardest to reconcile.

12

THE SPOOK

E than hated the Green Zone.

Not for any tactical reason—it was probably the safest square mile in Iraq, protected by blast walls and checkpoints and enough firepower to repel a division. He hated it because it was *comfortable*. Air conditioning. Real food. People in khakis and polo shirts walking around like they were at a conference center in McLean instead of the middle of a war zone.

He'd been summoned for a coordination meeting—something about integrating contractor intelligence products with official CIA reporting. Translation: someone at Langley wanted to make sure the contractors weren't stepping on the Agency's toes. Ethan, as the guy with a JD who could speak bureaucrat, got volunteered to represent MVM's interests.

Six months into his rotation now, and he was tired. His contract was up in a month. The bar exam was in three weeks, and he'd barely studied.

The meeting was exactly as tedious as he'd feared. Three hours in a conference room with too much air conditioning, listening to GS-14s talk about "deconfliction protocols" and "information sharing architectures." Ethan took notes, nodded at appropriate intervals, and tried not to think about the fact that while they were debating slide decks, people were getting shot at in Sadr City.

When it finally ended, he was in the hallway checking his phone—no signal, because of course not—when someone said, "You look like you need a drink."

Ethan turned. The guy was maybe his age, twenty-six or twenty-seven, with the kind of casual preppy look that screamed Ivy League: khakis, blue Oxford shirt rolled to the elbows, Timex watch, wire-rimmed glasses. He could have been interviewing at Goldman Sachs except for the CAC badge hanging around his neck that said "DOS" but definitely meant CIA.

"That obvious?" Ethan said.

"You had that look. Like you wanted to set the PowerPoint on fire." He extended a hand. "David Chen. Most people call me Dave."

"Ethan Caldwell." They shook. "And yeah, that was brutal."

"Tell me about it. I've been in country six months and I swear I've spent more time in meetings than running operations." Chen glanced at his watch. "You got a flight back to your FOB tonight?"

"Not till 0600 tomorrow. They stuck me in a CHU near the embassy."

"Perfect. Come on, I know a place."

The "place" turned out to be the Al-Rasheed Hotel, or what was left of it—a Saddam-era monstrosity that had been converted into a combination of quarters and social space for contractors and agency personnel. The bar, if you could call it that, was in a back room with a couple of couches and a folding table where someone had set up bottles of confiscated Iraqi whiskey and duty-free liquor from God knows where.

Chen poured two glasses of something amber that smelled like it might be actual scotch.

"To deconfliction," he said, raising his glass.

"To protocols," Ethan replied.

They drank. It was actual scotch—not great scotch, but real. Ethan felt some of the tension from the day start to dissolve.

"So," Chen said, settling into one of the couches. "MVM. You guys are doing the capture/kill analysis for the task forces, right?"

Ethan hesitated. "I can neither confirm nor—"

"Relax. I'm read into it. Plus, it's not exactly a secret. Everyone knows the contractors are embedded with JSOC elements." He paused. "I heard about some of your ops. Market snatch-and-grab in November. That firefight outside Baqubah in October. You've had an interesting rotation."

"You could say that." Ethan touched his scar unconsciously.

"That from Baqubah?"

"Yeah. Shrapnel."

Chen nodded. "I'm an operations officer. I run a network in Baghdad. Human intelligence."

There was something in how he said it—not quite an edge, but a distinction. Like HUMINT was somehow different from the kinetic work Ethan's world revolved around.

"Must be interesting," Ethan said neutrally.

"It is." Chen leaned back, swirling his drink. "You ever read le Carré? The old Cold War stuff?"

"Some. In college."

"That's what I thought this would be like. Recruiting assets. Dead drops. Running agents through hostile territory. The Great Game." He laughed, but it wasn't a happy sound. "Turns out it's mostly paying people for information that may or may not be true, then trying to figure out if they're playing you."

"Sounds familiar."

"Yeah? You guys have that problem too?"

"All the time," Ethan said. "We hit a house in November based on solid intel. Perfect operation. Right guy, clean capture, everything by the book. And somehow it still felt wrong."

Chen studied him. "That's interesting. Most people I talk to either don't think about it or convince themselves not to."

"Maybe I'm overthinking it."

"Or maybe you're thinking about it the right amount." Chen took a drink. "Can I ask you something? Off the record?"

"There is no record. We're drinking contraband whiskey in occupied Iraq."

"Do you ever wonder if we're doing the right thing?"

Ethan felt something loosen in his chest. Six months of firefights and perfect operations and moral ambiguity, and no one had asked him that directly. Not Ramos. Not Petey. Not even himself, not really.

"Every day," he said quietly.

Chen nodded. "I've got three sources in Baghdad. One's a former Republican Guard officer who hates Al-Qaeda more than he hates us. One's a kid, twenty years old, who needs money for his mother's medical bills. One's a sheikh in Adamiyah who plays all sides and is probably selling information to five different groups including us."

He took a drink. "The kid's my best source. Smart, motivated, takes risks. Last month he gave me intel that led to a raid—your guys, actually. They grabbed two AQI facilitators. Good outcome, right?"

"Right," Ethan said.

"Except now the kid's neighborhood knows he's been talking to Americans. He's had to move twice. His younger brother got jumped by militia thugs, put in the hospital. And the kid keeps showing up to meets because he needs the money, but I can see it in his eyes—he's terrified. And I keep running him because that's my job."

Chen looked at Ethan. "So yeah, I wonder if we're doing the right thing. I wonder if the information is worth what it costs the people who give it to us. I wonder if in ten years Iraq will be better or worse because we were here. And then I write my reports and meet my sources and pretend I have answers."

Ethan didn't know what to say. In all his time in Iraq, no one had been this honest. The operators treated it like a job. The intel guys focused on technical details. Even the other contractors kept things surface-level.

"You went to Harvard, right?" Chen said suddenly. "Kennedy School?"

"Just a one-week program. Executive education. Back in 2005, feels like a lifetime ago."

"Still counts." Chen smiled. "Yale, by the way. Class of '04. Poli sci major, Arabic minor, thought I was going to change the world. Applied to the Agency right after graduation, did the training, got sent here because I speak Arabic."

"How's that working out?"

"The Arabic? Helpful. The changing-the-world part?" He gestured at the room. "Jury's still out."

They drank in silence for a moment. Outside, Ethan could hear the distant thump of a helicopter, the white noise of generators.

"You know what the worst part is?" Chen said. "It's not the danger. It's not even the moral ambiguity. It's knowing that this is temporary. I'm here for eighteen months, then I rotate back to Langley, get assigned to some desk, eventually maybe get sent somewhere else. The kid I'm running? He's here forever. This is his life. We parachute in, play spy games, and leave. They have to live with whatever we do."

"That why you drink alone in the Al-Rasheed?"

"I'm not alone. You're here." Chen poured them both another glass. "Besides, drinking alone would be sad. Drinking with a fellow Ivy League guy who actually thinks about this stuff is just... I don't know, cathartic?"

"I'm a contractor," Ethan said. "Not CIA."

"Distinction without a difference. You analyze intelligence for kill/capture ops. You're embedded with classified units. You can't tell your family what you do. Sounds pretty CIA to me."

Ethan laughed despite himself. "That's a generous interpretation."

"It's an honest one." Chen's expression turned more serious. "Look, I don't know you. We've been talking for what, an hour? But I can tell you're thinking about this stuff. The right-and-wrong of it. Most people don't. Most people just do the job, cash the checks, tell themselves they're serving their country."

"And you don't think we are?"

"I think it's more complicated than that." Chen leaned forward. "Here's what I've learned in six months: there are no good guys in Iraq. Not really. There's us, there's Al-Qaeda, there's the militias, there's the government which is basically just another militia with better PR. Everyone's playing their own game. We tell ourselves we're here to help, to bring democracy, to fight terrorism. Maybe that's even true. But mostly we're here because we invaded and now we can't figure out how to leave without it looking like defeat."

"So what do we do?"

"We do our jobs," Chen said. "We run our sources, analyze our intel, write our reports. We try to make good calls with bad information. We try not to get anyone killed who doesn't deserve it—and sometimes we fail at that too. And maybe, if we're lucky, we do slightly more good than harm."

He raised his glass. "To slightly more good than harm."

Ethan clinked his glass against Chen's. "That's a pretty low bar."

"It's the only bar that matters."

They talked for another two hours. About Yale and Harvard, about how they'd both ended up in Iraq, about whether the war was winnable and what winning even meant. Chen told stories about his sources—the complicated ethics of running human beings as assets. Ethan talked about the operators he worked with, the chaos of the goat operation, the perfect capture that still felt wrong, the man in the grain field who still haunted his dreams.

Around midnight, Chen's phone buzzed. He checked it, grimaced.

"I've got a meet in an hour. One of my sources." He stood, stretched. "This was good. I don't get to talk like this much. Everyone's either too junior to understand or too senior to admit they have doubts."

"Yeah," Ethan said. "Same."

They walked back through the empty corridors of the Green Zone, past checkpoints staffed by bored contractors, past blast walls covered in graffiti.

"You know what's funny?" Chen said. "In another life, we probably would have ended up at the same law firm. Big corporate place in New York or DC. Making ridiculous money, working ridiculous hours, wondering if any of it mattered."

"Instead we're in Iraq."

"Instead we're in Iraq," Chen agreed. "Not sure if that's better or worse."

At the checkpoint where they had to split up—Chen heading to his meeting, Ethan back to his CHU—they shook hands.

"If you're ever back in the Green Zone, look me up," Chen said. "I'm here till July."

"I might not be back. Contract's up next month. Bar exam in three weeks."

"You taking it?"

"Flying back to Charleston for two days. Take the test, fly back out to finish the rotation, then... I don't know. Probably done after that."

Chen nodded. "Whatever you decide—whether to stay in, get out, go be a lawyer—make sure it's actually your decision. Not the Agency's, not the company's, not even your country's. Yours. Because at the end of the day, you're the one who has to live with it."

"Thanks," Ethan said, meaning it.

He watched Chen disappear into the darkness, heading to meet a terrified kid who was selling information for American money. Then he walked back to his CHU, lay down on his bunk, and stared at the ceiling.

In six hours he'd be on a helicopter back to his FOB. In three weeks he'd be taking the bar exam. In six weeks his contract would be up and he'd have to decide what came next.

But right now, for the first time in months, he didn't feel quite so alone.

He never saw David Chen again. The Green Zone was huge, their schedules didn't align, and his contract ended a month later. He tried to look Chen up once, years later, but CIA operations officers don't have LinkedIn profiles.

Sometimes, though, when Ethan saw news about Iraq—another bombing, another political crisis, another story about interpreters left behind—he thought about that night in the Al-Rasheed Hotel. About slightly more good than harm. About the kid with the sick mother who was probably still in Baghdad, still terrified, still trying to survive.

He wondered if Chen was still in the Agency. Still running sources. Still drinking contraband whiskey and wondering if any of it mattered.

And he wondered if Chen had found his answer.

Because Ethan was still looking for his.

Even years later, in a law office in Greenville, with the scar on his arm and the memories that wouldn't fade, he was still trying to figure out if they'd done slightly more good than harm.

The bar was low.

But maybe, Chen had been right, it was the only bar that mattered.

13

THE HANDOFF

E than sat in the plywood operations center, watching his replacement try to look comfortable in body armor that didn't quite fit. The kid—and he was a kid, maybe twenty-three—had the eager look of someone who thought Iraq was going to be an adventure. Fresh JD from Georgetown, some internship at State Department, probably thought he was going to change the world.

Ethan had looked like that once. Six months ago. A lifetime ago.

"So the detainee handling protocols are pretty straightforward," Ethan said, clicking through the PowerPoint he'd been told to prepare. "Geneva Conventions apply, even though we're contractors. New administration's really serious about this. More oversight, more documentation, more—"

"More bullshit," Ramos muttered from the back of the room, where he was ostensibly reviewing mission plans but actually listening to every word.

The kid—his name was Brandon, of course it was—looked nervous. "Is that... common? The, uh, attitude about regulations?"

"The attitude," Ethan said carefully, "is that we follow every regulation to the letter, because that's our job. But yeah, you're going to hear people complain. Ignore it. Do the paperwork. Cover your ass and theirs."

Brandon nodded, taking notes like this was a lecture at Georgetown instead of a briefing in a combat zone.

Ethan had been doing these handoff sessions for three days now—ever since the email from MVM's contract manager had arrived with the news. *Due to shifting operational priorities under the incoming administration, your contract will conclude on February 15, 2009. We appreciate your service and wish you well in future endeavors.*

Corporate-speak for: the new people in Washington don't want contractors doing this work anymore. Or at least, they want fewer contractors. Cheaper contractors. Different contractors. The details didn't matter. What mattered was that Ethan's rotation was ending a month early, and he was fine with that.

More than fine. Relieved, even.

The bar exam was February 24-25. He'd fly back to Charleston on the 16th, have a week to study, take the test, and then... figure out what came next. Greenville, probably. The small law firm. Estate planning and civil litigation. A life that didn't involve wondering if today was the day you got hit by an IED.

"What about the tactical side?" Brandon asked. "I mean, I know I'm here for legal oversight, but... do I need to know how to, you know..."

"Shoot?" Ramos supplied helpfully. "Clear a room? Tell the difference between an AK and an RPG?"

Brandon flushed. "I did some training. Basic stuff."

"He's asking if you've ever been in combat," Ethan translated. "And the answer's no, right?"

"Right."

Ethan exchanged a look with Ramos. The kid was going to learn fast, or he was going to be a liability. Probably both.

"Here's the thing," Ethan said, closing the PowerPoint. "Your job is to observe and document. That's it. You're not an operator. You're not a shooter. You're the guy who makes sure everything's by the book so that when Congress asks questions, we have answers."

"But what if something goes wrong? What if—"

"Then you stay down, don't get shot, and let the professionals do their job." Ethan stood up, gathering his notes. "Look, Brandon, I'm not trying to scare you. But this isn't Georgetown. People here are trying to kill us. Your job is to not make that easier for them."

After Brandon left—looking slightly less eager and considerably more nervous—Ramos lingered.

"Think he'll make it?" Ramos asked.

"Depends on whether he learns fast." Ethan said. "I didn't know anything when I got here either."

"You were different. You had instincts." Ramos paused. "You gonna miss this?"

Ethan looked around the operations center—plywood walls, PowerPoint slides about detainee protocols, maps of Baqubah marked with red circles indicating target compounds. Six months ago this had all been new and terrifying and somehow exciting. Now it just looked tired.

"No," he said honestly. "I don't think I will."

"Bullshit," Ramos said, but he was smiling. "You'll be in Greenville doing estate planning and you'll be bored out of your mind inside a month."

"Maybe." Ethan picked up his rifle—still his, for another three weeks—and headed for the door. "But at least I'll be bored somewhere people aren't trying to blow me up."

The next morning, Ethan found himself in the TOC during a mission brief he wasn't technically part of anymore. Old habits. Or maybe just avoiding his CHU, where his half-packed duffel bag sat like a reproach.

The target was a suspected AQI weapons cache in a village north of Baqubah. Standard raid. SEALs would hit the compound, SAD contractors would provide overwatch, and Brandon—sitting in the back taking nervous notes—would observe to make sure everything was legal.

"Counselor," the briefing officer said, noticing Ethan. "Didn't expect to see you here. Thought you were done?"

"Just observing," Ethan said. "Professional development for my replacement."

Brandon looked simultaneously grateful and terrified.

The op kicked off at 0300. Ethan watched from the TOC, monitoring radio traffic, tracking the team's progress on the tactical display. It was strange, being on this side of it. Hearing the voices without being there. Knowing what was happening without feeling it.

"Approaching objective," Ramos's voice crackled through the speaker.

"Copy," the TOC officer responded. "You are cleared hot."

Ethan found himself leaning forward, hands unconsciously clenched. Old instincts. He forced himself to relax.

The breach happened exactly on schedule. Then: "Contact! We got shooters in the compound!"

The radio exploded with controlled chaos—target calls, movement reports, casualty checks. Ethan's pulse kicked up even though he was miles away, safe in the TOC, not in danger.

Brandon looked like he might throw up.

"First time hearing that?" Ethan asked quietly.

"Yeah."

"Gets easier." Ethan didn't mention that it never really got easy. That even now, safe in the TOC, his body was remembering Baqubah, the culvert, the rounds snapping overhead, the man in the grain field.

The firefight lasted four minutes. One friendly wounded—not serious. Two enemy KIA. Weapons cache secured. Textbook operation.

"Good hit," the TOC officer said. "Clean work, Reaper-6."

Ethan realized he'd been holding his breath.

Later that day, he found Petey in the chow hall, eating something that might have been meatloaf.

"Heard you were in the TOC this morning," Petey said. "Babysitting the new guy?"

"Something like that." Ethan sat down with his own tray of questionable food. "How's the team taking it? The new guy, I mean."

"They'll adjust. Always do." Petey took a drink of what passed for coffee. "You adjusting?"

"To leaving? Yeah. It's time."

"That what you tell yourself?"

Ethan looked at him. "What's that supposed to mean?"

"Means you're in the TOC watching ops you're not part of anymore. Means you're still carrying your rifle everywhere even though you're not going outside the wire. Means you keep touching that scar like you're making sure it's still there."

Ethan stopped rubbing his arm. "I'm fine."

"Sure you are." Petey leaned back. "Look, I'm not saying you should stay. You got the law degree, you got options most of us don't. But don't kid yourself that this is gonna be easy to walk away from."

"It's not walking away. The contract ended."

"Because the new administration wants different priorities. Yeah, I heard." Petey's expression was unreadable. "But that's not why you're leaving, and we both know it."

Ethan wanted to argue, but Petey was right. The contract ending was convenient. It gave him an excuse. Made the choice for him, just like Chen had said it might.

Make sure it's actually your decision.

Was it? Or was he just letting circumstances decide for him?

"You remember that CIA guy I met?" Ethan said. "Chen. Operations officer."

"The Yale kid? Yeah."

"He told me to make sure whatever I decided was actually my decision. Not the Agency's, not the company's. Mine." Ethan pushed food around his tray. "I've been thinking about that."

"And?"

"And I think maybe he was right. I think... I think I'm leaving because I need to. Not because the contract's ending. That's just timing."

Petey nodded slowly. "Fair enough. But counselor? Don't beat yourself up if you miss it. This shit gets in your blood. Not the danger, not the adrenaline—though that's part of it. It's the... the clarity, I guess. Out here, things are simple. There's bad guys, there's us, and there's a job to do. Back in the world?" He shrugged. "Everything's complicated."

"Everything's already complicated," Ethan said quietly, thinking about Abu Khalil, about the good shoot that still felt wrong, about slightly more good than harm.

"Yeah," Petey agreed. "But out here, you can pretend it's not. That's the drug, counselor. That's what you're gonna miss."

Three days before his departure, there was a going-away thing in the team room. Not a party—nobody called it that—just the team, some contraband beer someone had smuggled in, and the kind of casual shit-talk that passed for affection among people who'd seen each other at their worst.

"To the counselor," Ramos said, raising a can. "Who spotted a gunman in Baghdad, survived Baqubah, and somehow managed to avoid shooting any civilians at Harvey Point."

"Low bar," Torres called out.

"It's counselor's bar," Kozlowski added. "He's into those."

Everyone laughed. Ethan found himself grinning despite everything.

"Seriously though," Ramos continued. "You came here a lawyer and you're leaving... well, still a lawyer, but one who knows which end of the rifle goes bang. That's something."

"Don't forget the goats," Hayes said. "He survived the goats."

"We all survived the goats," McKnight corrected. "Some of us with more dignity than others."

"It was a TACTICAL REPOSITIONING!"

The laughter rolled through the room, and Ethan felt something tight in his chest. These men—these operators and contractors and shooters—had become more than teammates. They'd become the people who knew things about him that he'd never be able to explain to anyone else.

How do you tell someone about the market, about the split-second decision to shout "Gun"? How do you explain Baqubah, the feeling of pulling the trigger and watching someone drop? How do you describe the strange alchemy that turned horror into humor, that made a ditch full of sewage and a goat attack into stories you laughed about?

You didn't. You couldn't. Not to people who hadn't been there.

"You gonna keep in touch?" Petey asked later, when the beer was gone and people were drifting back to their CHUs.

"Yeah," Ethan said. "I mean, probably. You guys know where to find me."

"Greenville, South Carolina. Practicing estate planning." Petey shook his head. "Never would've guessed that's where you'd end up when you first showed up here, all nervous and trying to act like you knew what you were doing."

"I had no idea what I was doing."

"None of us did, first time. You just figured it out faster than most." Petey extended his hand. "Take care of yourself, counselor. And if you ever need anything—anything at all—you know how to reach us."

They shook hands, and Ethan wondered if he'd ever see Petey again. Probably not. That's how these things worked. You spent months living in each other's pockets, closer than family, and then you went your separate ways and maybe exchanged Christmas cards for a few years before losing touch entirely.

It felt wrong. But then, a lot of things about leaving felt wrong.

His last mission—not really his, but he went along anyway, one more time—was a capture operation in a village west of Baqubah. Different compound, same drill. Brandon came too, his first real operation, looking like he might pass out.

The raid went smoothly. Target secured, no shots fired, textbook operation. On the ride back, Ethan watched Brandon trying to process it all—the controlled violence, the speed, the efficiency of trained operators doing what they did best.

"It's not what I expected," Brandon said quietly.

"What did you expect?"

"I don't know. More... chaos? You made it sound more dangerous."

"It is dangerous," Ethan said. "We just got lucky tonight. Ask me about Baqubah sometime. Ask me about the market. Ask me about—" He stopped. No point in traumatizing the kid before he even got started.

"The scar," Brandon said, nodding at Ethan's arm. "That from here?"

"Yeah."

"Does it hurt?"

"Sometimes. Mostly it just reminds me."

"Of what?"

Ethan looked out at the Iraqi darkness sliding past the MRAP's window. "Of the choices I made. The ones that were made for me. The difference between the two."

Brandon didn't ask what that meant. Probably for the best.

The day before his flight out, Ethan did a final walk through the FOB. It was smaller than he remembered from six months ago. Less imposing. Just plywood and sandbags and dust, not the overwhelming fortress it had seemed when he'd first arrived.

He stopped by the operations center, the chow hall, the range where he'd qualified. Each place held memories—some good, some not, most complicated. The weight of six months pressed down on him, and he realized he was saying goodbye not just to a place, but to a version of himself.

The version that had arrived here in August had been... what? Naive? Idealistic? Scared but trying not to show it? That Ethan had thought he understood what this work was. Thought his Harvard training and law degree made him qualified to observe operations and ensure everything was legal.

That Ethan had been an idiot.

The Ethan leaving in February knew things that Ethan couldn't unknow. Had seen things, done things, become someone he'd never planned to be.

In his CHU, he finished packing. Not much to take—some clothes, his notes, a few personal items. The important stuff wasn't physical.

It was in his head, his dreams, the way his hand still went to his rifle when he heard a loud noise, the way he automatically scanned rooms for threats.

There was a knock on his door. Ramos.

"Wanted to catch you before you left," Ramos said. "Figured you'd be up."

"Couldn't sleep."

"Never can, last night." Ramos leaned against the doorframe. "Look, I'm not good at this shit, so I'm just gonna say it. You were a good teammate, counselor. Better than good. You saved my ass in Baghdad, held your own in Baqubah, never complained, did your job. That matters."

"Thanks," Ethan said, not trusting himself to say more.

"And I know you're going back to be a lawyer and all that, but..." Ramos paused. "If you ever need anything. If things don't work out, or you get bored, or you just want to talk to someone who gets it. You have my number."

"I do."

"I mean it. We take care of our own. You're one of us now, whether you're here or in South Carolina doing will and estates or whatever the hell. That doesn't change."

After Ramos left, Ethan sat on his bunk and looked at his hands. They looked the same as they had six months ago, but they'd done things. Pulled triggers. Built breaching charges. Zip-tied detainees. Held the lives of teammates in split-second decisions.

These hands had killed someone.

That fact sat heavy on him, heavier than the body armor he wouldn't be wearing anymore, heavier than the rifle he was turning in tomorrow.

His phone buzzed—an email from his mother. *So excited to see you soon! Your room's all ready. We'll have a big dinner when you get home. Love you.*

Home. Savannah. His parents' house, where his bedroom still had his high school trophies and college textbooks. A place where none of this had happened, where he could pretend for a few days to be the person he'd been before.

Except he couldn't. That person was gone.

He typed back: *Looking forward to it. See you soon. Love you too.*

What he didn't type: *I killed someone. I'm good at things I never wanted to be good at. I don't know if I did more good than harm. I don't know if I can go back to being a lawyer. I don't know who I am anymore.*

Some things you couldn't say. Not to your mother. Not to anyone who hadn't been here.

The flight out was on a C-17, packed with soldiers and Marines rotating home, all of them loud and relieved and ready to be gone. Ethan sat quietly in the red light of the cargo bay, his duffel between his feet, and watched Iraq disappear below the clouds.

Somewhere down there, the team was already planning the next operation. Brandon was learning the rhythm. The war was continuing without him.

And somewhere—maybe in Baghdad, maybe rotated back to Langley by now—Chen was running his sources, paying his terrified kid for information, wondering if they were doing slightly more good than harm.

Make sure it's actually your decision.

He'd thought the contract ending made the choice for him. But sitting on this plane, leaving Iraq behind, he realized Chen had been wrong about one thing. It wasn't about whether the decision was his. It was about whether he could live with it.

Could he go back to being a lawyer? Could he sit in an office in Greenville and draft wills and settle estates and pretend he hadn't learned how to clear rooms and build breaching charges and read situations for threats?

Could he be the person his parents thought he was, the person Sterling had mentored, the person who'd graduated from Charleston Law with dreams of public service?

He didn't know.

But the plane was banking west, toward Charleston, toward the bar exam, toward a life that didn't involve gunfire and raids and the weight of choices made in darkness.

The choice had been made. Whether it was his or not didn't matter anymore.

He closed his eyes and tried to sleep, but all he saw was the man in the grain field, the red dot sight, the figure dropping. All he heard was Chen's voice: *slightly more good than harm.*

The bar was low.

But it was the only bar that mattered.

And as Iraq fell away beneath him, Ethan Caldwell wondered if he'd ever know whether he'd cleared it.

—-

Charleston, South Carolina – February 16, 2009

The humidity hit him like a wall when he stepped off the plane at Charleston. After six months of Iraqi desert, the Lowcountry felt impossibly green, impossibly humid, impossibly alive.

His parents met him at the airport. His mother cried. His father shook his hand firmly, the way men of his generation did, and Ethan saw something in his father's eyes—recognition, maybe, or understanding. The look of someone who'd served himself, decades ago, and knew what wasn't being said.

"Welcome home, son," his father said.

Home. The word felt foreign.

They drove to Savannah, his mother talking the whole way about neighbors and family and plans for his homecoming dinner. Ethan made appropriate noises, nodded at the right times, and watched the South Carolina landscape roll past—so different from Iraq, so familiar, so strange.

That night, in his childhood bedroom, surrounded by the artifacts of a life that felt like it belonged to someone else, Ethan opened his laptop and started studying for the bar exam.

Eight days. That's all he had. Eight days to cram six months of absence into his brain, to remember contracts and torts and civil procedure when all his mind wanted to do was replay operations and firefights and the sound of Yousef falling into the ditch.

His phone rang. Unknown number. He almost didn't answer.

"Counselor." Ramos's voice. "Just checking in. You make it home okay?"

"Yeah. I'm good."

"Bullshit. Nobody's good their first night back. But you will be. Give it time."

"How much time?"

"However long it takes." A pause. "You got people there? People you can talk to?"

"My parents. Some friends from law school, I guess."

"That's not what I meant."

Ethan knew what he meant. People who'd been there. People who understood. And the answer was no. He didn't have anyone like that in Charleston or Savannah. Just his team, scattered across the world, living their own complicated lives.

"I'll be fine," Ethan said.

"Yeah. You will." Ramos sounded like he actually believed it. "Good luck on that bar exam, counselor. You're gonna crush it."

After they hung up, Ethan sat in the silence of his childhood bedroom and listened to the sounds of suburban Savannah at night—cars on the street, neighbors' televisions, the hum of air conditioning. So different from the generators and helicopters and distant explosions of Iraq.

He opened his bar exam prep materials and tried to focus on the rule against perpetuities.

All he could think about was slightly more good than harm.

The bar was low.

But first, he had to pass the actual bar.

He smiled at the thought—his first genuine smile since leaving Iraq—and got to work.

The war was over. For him, at least.

Now came the harder part: figuring out how to live with what he'd learned.

14

THE CALL

Ethan Caldwell's phone rang at 2:47 AM, pulling him from a dream about grain fields and red dot sights. Six years since Iraq, and he still had those dreams. Less often now—maybe once a month instead of every night—but they never really went away.

He grabbed the phone from his nightstand, squinting at the unknown number. Probably a wrong number. Or a client emergency, though those were rare in estate planning.

"This is Ethan," he said, his voice rough with sleep.

"Counselor." The voice was familiar but older, weathered. "It's Ramos."

Ethan sat up, suddenly fully awake. He hadn't heard from Ramos i n... three years? Maybe four? They'd kept in touch after Iraq—Christmas cards, occasional emails, one awkward beer in Charlotte when Ramos was passing through—but eventually the contact had faded. That's how these things went.

"Ramos. Jesus, it's been—"

"Too long, I know." Ramos didn't sound social. He sounded tired. "Look, I wouldn't be calling like this if it wasn't important. You still practicing law in Greenville?"

"Yeah. Same firm, six years now. Why?"

A pause. Long enough that Ethan wondered if the connection had dropped.

"I need a lawyer," Ramos said finally. "And I need someone who understands... what we did. What it was like. Someone who won't ask the wrong questions."

Ethan's pulse kicked up, old instincts activating. "What kind of trouble are you in?"

"Not me. A friend. Former teammate." Another pause. "It's Yousef."

The name hit Ethan like a physical thing. Yousef. The terp from the ditch incident. The literature professor turned interpreter who'd survived Iraq by speaking English and Arabic and knowing when to laugh at himself.

"Yousef," Ethan repeated. "From Baghdad?"

"Yeah. He's here. In the States. Been here since 2011, got his SIV finally after three years of paperwork. He's in Charlotte now, working as a translator, trying to build a life." Ramos's voice went flat. "And now ICE has him in detention. They're saying his visa application had irregularities. They're talking about deportation."

Ethan was already reaching for his laptop. "What kind of irregularities?"

"Does it matter? It's bullshit. He risked his life for us for four years. Took two bullets in Ramadi in '09 after you left. His brother was killed by AQI for working with Americans. And now some bureaucrat in immigration is saying he lied on his application about... I don't even know what. Something about his employment history or his family connections or some other bullshit."

Ethan opened his computer, the blue light harsh in his dark bedroom. "Ramos, I do estate planning and civil litigation. Immigration law is a completely different—"

"I know. But you understand what he did. What it cost him. And you're a lawyer. You know other lawyers. You can help."

"There are immigration attorneys in Charlotte who specialize in—"

"I already called three of them." Ramos's voice was tight with frustration. "They all said the same thing. Special Immigrant Visa cases are complicated. The immigration court backlog is years long. Best case, it's a long shot. Worst case, he's on a plane back to Iraq in six months."

"And then what? AQI is gone but ISIS is everywhere now. They keep lists. Terps, translators, anyone who worked with Americans. You know what they do to guys like Yousef."

Ethan did know. He'd seen the reports. Read the stories. Watched the news footage of mass executions and beheadings. Iraq in 2015 was worse than Iraq in 2008, if that was even possible.

"Where is he being held?" Ethan asked.

"Stewart Detention Center. Georgia. About three hours from you."

Ethan looked at his clock. 2:51 AM. He had a will signing at 10 AM. A consultation about a personal injury case at 2 PM. A completely normal day of completely normal legal work that paid his rent and his student loans and kept his life uncomplicated.

"I'll need to see his file," Ethan heard himself say. "Everything. The original SIV application, the visa itself, the ICE detention paperwork, any correspondence about the irregularities they're claiming."

"I can get you that. How soon can you get down there?"

"Tomorrow. Today, I mean." Ethan was already mentally rearranging his schedule. "I'll need to clear my appointments, but I can be there by afternoon."

"Thank you." Ramos's voice cracked slightly. "I know this isn't your area, I know I'm asking a lot, but—"

"He fell in a ditch," Ethan said quietly. "Remember? Outside Baqubah. He fell in that sewage ditch and we gave him shit about it all night."

"Yeah." Ramos's laugh was brief and sad. "Yeah, I remember."

"He was part of the team. We don't leave team behind."

After they hung up, Ethan sat in his dark bedroom and stared at his laptop screen. His reflection looked back at him from the darkened monitor—thirty-two years old, six years removed from Iraq, living a quiet life in Greenville doing quiet legal work for quiet clients.

The scar on his left arm itched.

He touched it unconsciously, feeling the raised tissue through his t-shirt. He hadn't thought about that scar in months. Hadn't dreamed about the grain field in weeks. Had almost convinced himself that Iraq was just something that had happened once, long ago, to a different version of himself.

Almost.

The next morning, Ethan called his senior partner from his car, already on I-85 heading south toward Georgia.

"Family emergency," he said, which wasn't quite a lie. "I need to cancel today's appointments. Maybe tomorrow's too."

"Everything okay?" Margaret Chen—no relation to David—was sixty-three and had been practicing law in Greenville since before Ethan was born. She'd hired him in 2009, fresh off passing the bar, probably because she felt sorry for him. Six years later, she was still the best boss he'd ever had.

"Yeah. Old friend needs help. Legal issue."

"What kind of legal issue?"

"Immigration."

There was a pause. Margaret knew Ethan didn't do immigration work. She also knew—because he'd told her during his initial interview, in the vaguest possible terms—that he'd done "consulting work overseas" before law school. She'd never pressed for details.

"You sure you know what you're doing?" she asked.

"Not even slightly."

"Okay. Keep me posted. And Ethan? If you need help—referrals, co-counsel, anything—call me."

"Thanks, Margaret."

He drove through the October morning, watching the South Carolina landscape give way to Georgia. The radio played news about Syria, about ISIS, about the refugee crisis in Europe. About immigration reform and border security and all the complicated ways America was trying to figure out what it owed to the people who'd helped it fight its wars.

His phone rang again. Different number, but he recognized it this time.

"Petey," Ethan said, putting it on speaker.

"Heard you're riding to the rescue." Petey sounded amused. "Ramos called me this morning. Said you're going full white knight for Yousef."

"I'm going to look at his file and see if there's anything I can do. That's it."

"That's more than anyone else was willing to do." Petey paused. "You know this is going to be a shitshow, right? Immigration cases are nightmares. SIV cases are worse. And if ICE has already decided to push deportation..."

"I know."

"But you're doing it anyway."

"Yeah."

"Good man." Petey's voice went serious. "Look, I'm still in the game. Still contracting, different company, different theater. But I've got contacts. People at State, people at DHS, people who might be able to make calls. You need anything—anything at all—you let me know."

"I will."

"And counselor? It's good to hear from you. Even if it takes Yousef getting fucked by the system to make it happen."

After Petey hung up, Ethan thought about the last six years. He'd built a good life in Greenville. Small apartment, respectable job, a few friends from the local bar association. He dated occasionally, nothing serious. Went to the gym, played pickup basketball, had a standing Thursday night poker game with some guys from law school.

It was a normal life. A good life.

It was also, if he was being honest, kind of boring.

Not boring like "I wish I was getting shot at again." Boring like... quiet. Safe. Uncomplicated. The kind of life where the biggest stress was whether a client's will properly accounted for their grandchildren's trust fund.

He'd wanted that after Iraq. Craved it. The simplicity, the safety, the sense that his actions had clear consequences and clean outcomes.

But somewhere along the way, that safety had started to feel like stagnation.

Stewart Detention Center was a low, institutional building that looked exactly like what it was—a privately-run immigration prison in the middle of rural Georgia. Ethan showed his bar card, went through security, and waited in a consultation room that smelled like industrial cleaner and despair.

When they brought Yousef in, Ethan almost didn't recognize him.

The man from Baghdad had been stocky, energetic, quick with a joke even covered in sewage. This Yousef was thinner, grayer, wearing an orange jumpsuit that hung loose on his frame. But his eyes—his eyes were the same. Sharp. Intelligent. Exhausted.

"Counselor," Yousef said, and smiled. "I heard you became a real lawyer."

"I heard you fell in a ditch," Ethan replied, standing to shake his hand.

Yousef's laugh was brief but genuine. "I heard you watched and did nothing while I suffered."

"We hosed you down. That was something."

They sat across from each other at the metal table, and for a moment neither spoke. Six years. A lifetime. A world away from Iraq.

"Ramos called me," Ethan said finally. "Told me about your situation. I've reviewed your file—what I could get my hands on so far. You want to tell me your version?"

Yousef's smile faded. "My version is I did everything right. Applied for the SIV in 2008, after you left. Took three years to process. Three years hiding in Baghdad, moving every few months because AQI had my name on a list. My brother..." He stopped, collected himself. "My brother was killed in 2010. They found him because of me. Because he had the same family name."

"I'm sorry," Ethan said.

"I finally got the visa in 2011. Came here, to Charlotte. Worked as a translator for a refugee resettlement agency. Learned to drive on the wrong side of the road. Learned to say 'soda' instead of 'fizzy drink.' Tried to become American." Yousef's hands were flat on the table, steady despite everything. "And then two months ago, ICE agents came to my apartment. Said there were irregularities in my application. Said I might have lied about my employment history, about whether I'd ever been a member of a terrorist organization, about—" He stopped. "It's bullshit. All of it."

"What specifically are they claiming?"

"They say I failed to disclose that I worked for an Iraqi government ministry before I became an interpreter. They say that ministry had ties to insurgent groups. They say that makes me a security risk." Yousef's voice was carefully controlled. "I worked as a translator for the Ministry of Culture. I translated French poetry. I had nothing to do with insurgents."

Ethan took notes. "Did you disclose that employment on your SIV application?"

"Yes. It's in the paperwork. They just... they're choosing to interpret it differently now."

"Why now? Why after four years?"

Yousef shrugged. "Politics? Quotas? Someone decided to review old cases and found one they could challenge?" He leaned forward. "Counselor, I'm not naive. I know what's happening. The climate has changed. Politicians want to look tough on immigration. And refugees from Iraq, even ones who helped Americans, are easy targets."

Ethan thought about the news he'd been hearing. The presidential campaign already ramping up. The rhetoric about borders and security and vetting. The way "refugee" had become a political football.

"I need to be honest with you," Ethan said. "This isn't my specialty. I do estate planning. Wills, trusts, some civil litigation. I've never handled an immigration case."

"But you understand what I did. What it cost." Yousef's eyes held his. "Ramos says you're the only lawyer he knows who won't just see this as another case. Who'll understand why it matters."

"It matters," Ethan said quietly. "You saved lives. Ours. Other teams'. You put yourself and your family at risk to help us. That matters."

"Will it matter to the judge?"

Ethan didn't answer immediately. He thought about his six years in Greenville, doing quiet legal work. He thought about the man in the grain field, about slightly more good than harm, about all the ways he'd tried to convince himself that Iraq was over and done with.

"I don't know," he said honestly. "But I'm going to find out."

That night, in a cheap hotel near the detention center, Ethan called Margaret.

"I need help," he said. "Immigration law. Specifically Special Immigrant Visa cases and removal proceedings. You know anyone?"

"I know someone who knows someone." Margaret paused. "You're really doing this?"

"Yeah."

"Okay. Give me until tomorrow morning. I'll make some calls."

"Margaret? Thank you."

"Don't thank me yet. Immigration cases are hard. SIV cases are harder. And if ICE is pushing deportation..." She didn't finish the sentence. She didn't need to.

After they hung up, Ethan opened his laptop and started researching. Immigration law was a maze of statutes, regulations, case precedents, and administrative procedures. Special Immigrant Visas had their own additional layer of complexity—State Department oversight, security clearances, military documentation requirements.

It would take months to become competent in this area. Maybe years.

He didn't have months.

His phone buzzed. A text from a number he didn't recognize: *Heard you're helping Yousef. Let me know if you need anything. Still owe you for Baghdad. - Kozlowski*

Another text, different number: *Ramos told me. I've got some contacts at State from my contracting days. Happy to make introductions. - Torres*

Another: *Whatever you need, counselor. Yousef was good people. - McKnight*

Ethan stared at his phone. The team. Six years later, scattered across the country, living different lives. But still a team.

He thought about what Ramos had said that last night in Iraq: *We take care of our own.*

At 11 PM, his phone rang. Unknown number. Again.

"This is Ethan."

"Counselor." The voice was different but familiar. Educated. Tired. "This is David Chen. You might not remember me—"

"I remember." Ethan sat up straighter. "The Al-Rasheed Hotel. January 2009. Contraband scotch and a conversation about whether we were doing the right thing."

"Good memory." Chen sounded surprised. "I heard through the grapevine—and by grapevine I mean Petey, who apparently knows everyone—that you're helping a terp with a deportation case."

"Yousef. Yeah. You know him?"

"Different AO, but I know the type. Smart guys who spoke English and took impossible risks for not enough money." Chen paused. "I'm at Langley now. Middle East desk. I've got some friends at State and DHS who might be willing to make calls, write letters, vouch for the value of SIV holders. If you think that would help."

"Why?" Ethan asked. "Why would you do that?"

"Because I'm still running sources in Iraq. Still paying people for information that might get them killed. Still wondering if we're doing slightly more good than harm." Chen's voice was quiet. "And because guys like Yousef are the reason any of what we did mattered. If we don't take care of them, what the hell was the point?"

After Chen hung up, Ethan sat in his hotel room and realized what was happening. The team was reassembling. Not physically, but functionally. Ramos, Petey, Kozlowski, Torres, McKnight, Chen. All of them reaching out, offering help, calling in favors.

For Yousef. For the guy who fell in the ditch.

Because that's what you did. You took care of your own.

Ethan opened his laptop and started drafting a memo. He didn't know immigration law, but he knew how to research. He knew how to build an argument. He knew how to fight.

And he knew that six years of estate planning in Greenville had been... what? Not wasted, exactly. But not what he was meant to do. Not really.

The call had come at 2:47 AM. A voice from the past, asking for help.

And Ethan Caldwell, estate planning attorney from Greenville, South Carolina, had said yes.

Because some doors never fully closed. Some wars never really ended. And some debts could never be repaid—you could only try to honor them.

Outside his hotel window, the Georgia night was quiet and dark. Tomorrow he'd go back to the detention center. He'd start building Yousef's case. He'd call Margaret's contacts and learn immigration law from scratch. He'd fight ICE and the immigration courts and all the bureaucratic machinery that had decided a literature professor who'd survived Iraq wasn't worth keeping.

It would be hard. It would probably fail. The odds were terrible.

But slightly more good than harm.

That was the bar. The only bar that mattered.

And Ethan Caldwell was finally ready to clear it.

He rubbed the scar on his left arm, smiled, and got back to work.

The quiet life could wait.

Right now, he had a job to do.

—-

Three Months Later – January 2016

The courtroom in Atlanta was nothing like Ethan had imagined. No drama, no passionate speeches, just a tired immigration judge, a government attorney who looked bored, and Yousef in a suit that Ramos had bought him, sitting quietly at the defense table.

Ethan had spent three months learning immigration law. Margaret had connected him with an experienced immigration attorney named Sarah Patel who'd agreed to serve as co-counsel. Together, they'd built a case: letters from Ramos, Petey, and a dozen other operators vouching for Yousef's service. Documentation from MVM and the CIA confirming his role. A letter from David Chen at Langley, carefully worded but clear in its support.

And a 47-page brief that Ethan had written himself, arguing that the "irregularities" ICE claimed were either administrative errors or intentional mischaracterizations of disclosed information.

"Mr. Caldwell," the judge said, "I've reviewed your brief. It's thorough. Perhaps excessively so."

"Your Honor, my client risked his life for four years helping American forces in Iraq. His brother was killed because of that service. I don't think any brief defending his right to remain in this country can be excessive."

The judge—a woman in her fifties who'd probably heard a thousand cases just like this—looked at Yousef. "Mr. Al-Tamimi, do you have anything you'd like to say?"

Yousef stood. "Your Honor, I didn't come to America because it was easy. I came because I believed in what we were trying to do in Iraq. Democracy, freedom, a better future. I believed that enough to risk everything." He paused. "I still believe it. I want to be American. I want to contribute. I want to build a life here. Please don't send me back to a country where my name is on an execution list."

The judge was quiet for a long moment. Then: "The government's case relies heavily on the petitioner's alleged failure to disclose employment with an Iraqi ministry that had alleged ties to insurgent groups. However, the documentation provided by Mr. Caldwell shows that this employment was in fact disclosed, and that the ministry in question—the Ministry of Culture—has no established connection to insurgent activity." She looked at the government attorney. "Unless you have evidence to the contrary?"

The government attorney shuffled papers. "Your Honor, we believe the totality of the circumstances—"

"Yes or no, counselor. Do you have evidence that the Ministry of Culture was connected to insurgent groups?"

"No, Your Honor."

The judge nodded. "Then I'm granting the motion to terminate removal proceedings. Mr. Al-Tamimi, your visa status is restored. Welcome to America."

Outside the courthouse, Yousef grabbed Ethan in a hug that would have been embarrassing if Ethan hadn't been too relieved to care.

"Thank you," Yousef said, his voice thick. "Thank you, thank you—"

"Thank the team," Ethan said. "They're the ones who made the calls, wrote the letters, vouched for you."

"I'm thanking them too. But you're the one who spent three months learning a new area of law to save my ass." Yousef stepped back, wiping his eyes. "The guy who watched me fall in a ditch and laughed."

"We hosed you down after."

"After you laughed."

They stood on the courthouse steps, two men who'd survived Iraq in different ways, and for a moment neither spoke.

"What now?" Ethan asked finally. "You going back to Charlotte?"

"Eventually. First I need to call my wife—I got married, can you believe it? American woman, teacher, met her at the refugee center—and tell her I'm not getting deported." Yousef smiled. "Then I need to find the rest of the team and thank them. And then..." He paused. "Then I need to live a life worthy of all this. Of my brother's sacrifice. Of everyone who helped me. Of the second chance I just got."

After Yousef left, Ethan sat on the courthouse steps and called Margaret.

"We won," he said.

"I heard. Sarah Patel called me. She said you did good work. Said you're a natural at immigration law."

"I'm not doing immigration law. I'm coming back to estate planning."

"Are you?" Margaret's voice was knowing. "Because from where I'm sitting, you just spent three months more alive than I've seen you in six years."

Ethan didn't have an answer for that.

"Think about it," Margaret said. "You've got options now. You've always had options. But maybe it's time to figure out which ones actually make you happy."

—-

Greenville, South Carolina – February 2016

Ethan sat in his apartment, looking at his laptop. He'd been back from Atlanta for two weeks. Back to his regular cases, his regular life, his regular routine.

It felt wrong. Too quiet. Too safe. Too much like he was wasting something.

His phone rang. Ramos.

"Saw the news about Yousef," Ramos said. "Hell of a thing you did, counselor."

"We did. Team effort."

"Yeah, but you're the one who made it happen." Ramos paused. "So what's next?"

"What do you mean?"

"I mean, are you going back to estate planning? Or are you going to do something with what you just learned?"

Ethan looked around his apartment. Neat. Organized. Empty.

"I don't know," he said honestly.

"Well, when you figure it out, let me know. Because I know about three other terps in similar situations. And there's probably a hundred more who could use someone who gives a shit and knows what they're doing."

After they hung up, Ethan opened his laptop and started researching. Immigration attorneys who specialized in SIV cases. Organizations that helped refugees. Legal aid clinics that needed volunteers.

He thought about Chen's question from six years ago: *Do you ever wonder if we're doing the right thing?*

He thought about the answer: *Slightly more good than harm.*

He thought about Yousef, married now, building a life, living free because someone had been willing to fight for him.

Maybe that was the answer. Maybe that was what the last six years had been preparing him for. Not estate planning. Not hiding from Iraq in a quiet life in Greenville.

But using what he'd learned—both in law school and in Iraq—to help the people who'd helped him. To clear the bar that Chen had set. To do slightly more good than harm.

It wasn't a plan. Not yet.

But it was a start.

Ethan rubbed his scar, smiled, and got to work.

The call had come three months ago. He'd answered.

And now, maybe, he was finally ready for whatever came next.

15

ACKNOWLEDGMENT

*T*his novel was inspired by the experiences of contractors, soldiers, and interpreters who served in Iraq during the surge and drawdown years. While all characters are fictional, they reflect the real complexity of war, service, and the choices we make in impossible situations.